SUITCASE B

Little Jack Horner
A novel by Peter Kalu

ISBN 978-1-905778-05-8

Little Jack Horner

Published 2007 by Suitcase

Copyright © Peter Kalu 2007

The right of Peter Kalu to be identified as the author of this work has been asserted by her in accordance with the Copyright, Designs and Patents Act 1988

This work is entirely a work of fiction and any resemblance to persons living or dead or to companies or authorities is purely coincidental.

No part of this publication may be reproduced without written permission except in the case of brief extracts embodied in critical articles, reviews or lectures. For further information contact Suitcase Books

admin@suitcasebooks.info
www.suitcasebooks.info

Suitcase Books are published by
Shorelines: info@shorelines.org.uk

Suitcase books are distributed by Turnaround Publisher Services Ltd, Unit 3, Olympia Trading Estate, Coburg Rd, Wood Green, London N22 6TZ

Cover design by Ian Bobb (07799137492)
Printed by LPPS Limited, 128 Northampton Rd, Wellingborough, NN8 3PJ, UK

British Library Cataloguing-in-Publication Data. A catalogue record for this book is available from the British Library

Little Jack Horner

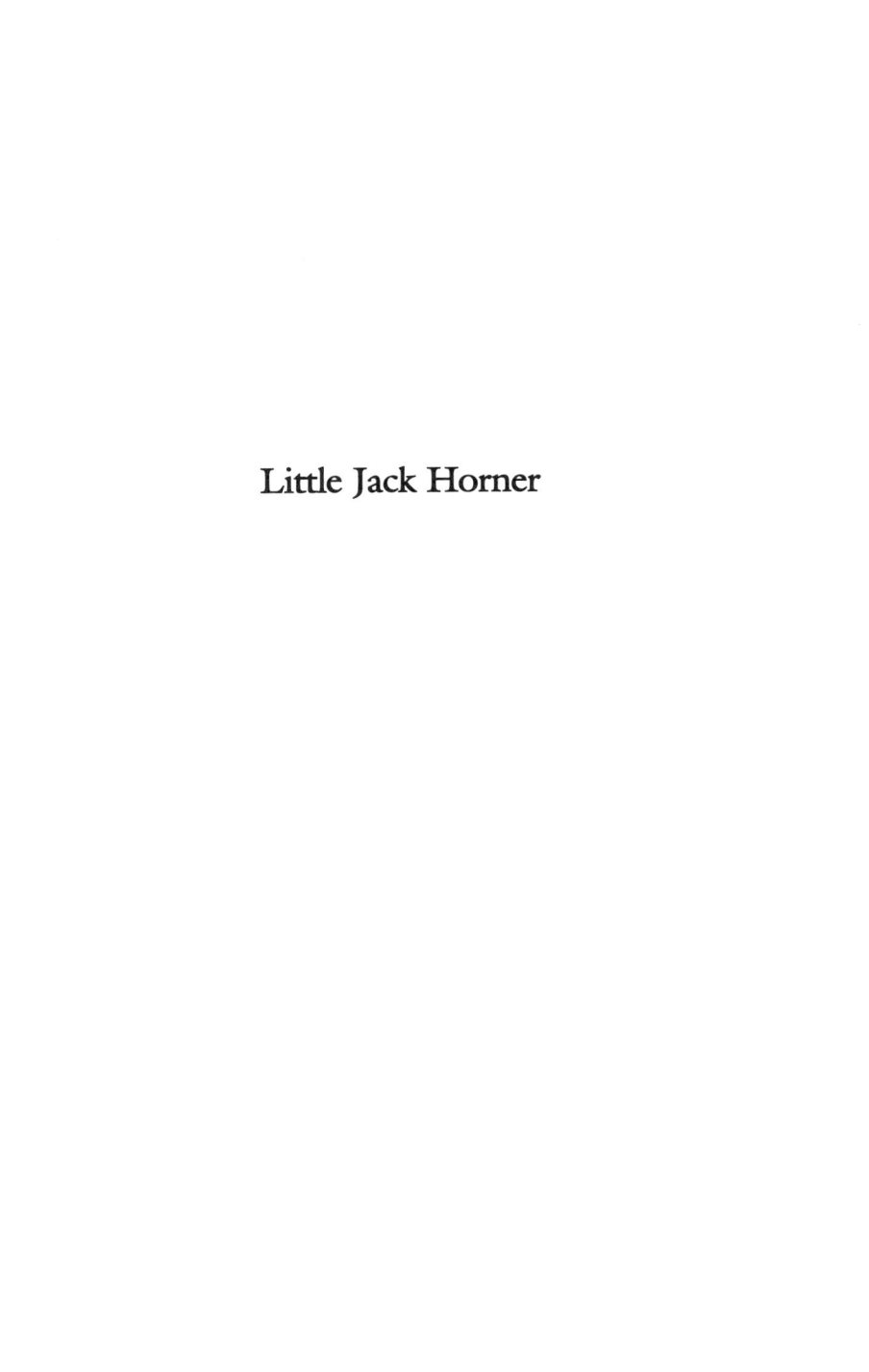

To Stephen
and all the
nephews and nieces

I

1

A weak November sun pushed through the dirt filmed high window of Amin High Street Carpets, glanced off the peeling Islamic prayer mirror that hung on the high shop interior wall, and scattered weak pools of pale light downwards, dappling the blue, industrial cord carpet floor where a bored Karim Amin was scuffing his shoes.

With the warehouse closed, they were holding all their stock here. Roll on roll of carpet leaned proudly on walls, soared into the roof space. The cocktail of smells soothed Karim: the heavy fumes of rubber underlay, the lighter sniff of the foam backeds, the classy aroma of the wool twists and Berbers, the wincing snort of the cheaper nylons; all wafted and mingled by the shop's cranky central heating. And did he imagine it or could he also detect his father's loose leaf tea, the chappati and dahl they had shared for lunch and, lurking low, the sour goat's milk of his damp Nike trainers? 'You have an over-educated nose,' Karim thought to himself. 'And an undereducated brain, Karim!' he imagined Mr Millar, his ex-college tutor joining in with a scowl. Karim was not short of critics.

He looked across at his bear of a father. Pops needed to diet. His dad was ancient – at least sixty-two years old, perhaps even seventy. No one was sure of the exact age because his passport age was just a guess. Karim wanted him to lose at least a stone. When he fetched their lunch every day from Marhaba, Karim had the cooks drawing off the excess ghee and not buttering the nan bread. His father complained the cooks were skimping and did they take him for a fool, thank goodness for your mother and he would eat fish, chips and mushy peas rather than put up with this dry nan, dry as a river bed during drought!

The ideal, Karim thought would be to get Pops on a treadmill. The only exercise he currently took was from the door of his ageing Mercedes to the door of their carpet shop, and now he had the shape of many old Punjabi men. His stomach was ten centimetres ahead of his nose when he came through a door, and it pushed upwards into his chest. His legs were still strong at the thigh, but spindly below the knee. Karim did not like to see his dad lift carpets onto customers' roof racks or into taxis any more. The weight of an average hessian-backed carpet – a five by five Wilton for instance – would burst his fatty heart one day. His father claimed he felt no strain, but Karim had seen the glaze on his face as he hefted a carpet onto his shoulder; seen that glaze become a sweaty torrent as he staggered with it, his mouth set in a deathly grimace, towards the customer's vehicle. The last time it had happened, Karim had hung the Closed sign up and blasted him – threatened to go back to college – warehouse burn down or no warehouse burn down. His father had raged, but finally relented: while Karim was working in the shop his dad never lifted carpets. And he'd been true to his word. One of the few of their battles Karim had won. He was determined his dad was not going to die on him any time soon. For one, Mum would never recover. He still remembered his mum at granddad's funeral. All that wailing. Then tears every morning for months.

It was a lazy, late Friday afternoon, almost closing. The shop had been quiet all day. His older brother, Shafiq, was out in the van, touring wholesalers. It beat sitting in the shop watching dust circling. Dad and Shafiq ran the shop, but they were barely on speaking terms. Shafiq thought, wrongly, that Dad blamed him for the fire – an electrical fault in a storage heater – but they were pulling in different directions anyway on which way the business should go. The fire was one and a half years ago and Dad had under-insured. They had to sell off the warehouse building and switch Shafiq to the driving job. For two years Dad had been seeing bankruptcy advisors. 'Trading Insolvently' his accountants had pronounced before Dad sacked them. Only now had the banks stopped ringing daily.

His dad called out to him:

-Karim, what are the advantages of cord carpet over linoleum?

-Cord is softer on the feet, looks better, more civilised, Dad.

-What are the advantages of Axminster over cord carpet?

-Harder wearing. Warms the house. They put it in castles, mansions and stately homes.

-What are the advantages of Wilton over Axminster?

-The Queen of England walks on these. They lay it in Buckingham Palace, Five Star Hotels, the Taj Mahal.

-Good. What are the advantages...

Karim rested at his small, clear varnished pine table looking across at his father who was sat at the battered oak desk with the cash till and orders spike. When things were quiet his dad liked to grill him like this. Sales training he called it. Karim knew the answers off by heart – five months repetition had seen to that. It was centuries out of date sales thinking, but it pleased his father; they could have been reciting prayers, so well did they each know the lines.

-Karim, are you a goldfish? Concentrate now. What are the advantages of wool twist over man-made?

-Easy...

His father's face was like the dial pad of a push button table telephone. Or the inside of a sliced pomegranate. Or the surface of an old pineapple. The pockmarks were strangely regular, so a blind man feeling his face would be confused that maybe there was a hidden message in Braille or Morse there. His eyes were what Karim admired most. Why had he not inherited them? While his own eyes were wide and open and bafflingly cute no matter how mean he tried to look, his father's eyes had the narrow, arrow-shaped swagger of an '80s Bollywood movie star. His thick, silvery moustache completed the effect. Without the pocks on his face, he might have had a chance at stardom if he had been born into a Delhi film dynasty and not a tribe of carpet sellers from Peshawar.

-Karim, why do you young people not come into the carpet shop? I don't see one in three months. Nobody getting married, setting up house?

-They want wood floors now.

-What? his father exclaimed, incredulous.

-It's good business. Houses here are as old as dinosaurs. Floorboards are wonky, all covered in paint, dust and stuff. So they take up the carpet and they put new flooring over the old floor. New wood floor.

-Isn't it expensive?

-Not laminate. Looks like new wood.

-Why do they want to do that? Their feet will raw without carpet.

-Nah, it's warm, you put insulation under. All the soap characters have it now. East Enders. Coronation Street. Wood laminate. It's... the new Axminster.

-Strange, his father wondered out loud.

-It's modern. It's warm and no carpet bugs therefore no asthma. Spills just wipe up and it makes a room look bigger. At the cheap end, the price is the same as good carpet.

-I am a modern man, son. We must think about stocking this laminate. Where do they put it? Lounge? Bathroom?

It was good to see Dad's face light up again. Since the fire he had been carpeting all hours. It was like a mania. He would talk to you any place, any time so long as it was carpets. And after the fire, everything was insured to the hilt. He'd even bought an electronic gizmo from B&Q and tested every appliance, shop and home, monthly, in a solemn ritual. One evening Karim was wanking under the blankets when his dad walked in. Pops just carried on to the sockets with the electrical tester, plugged the tester in, checked the reading and walked out again. Glided in and out without a beat while he had been rubbing himself furiously.

Idly, Karim watched the yellow Burnham Evening News van pull up and the driver whip the latest Burnham Evening Chronicle headline sheet into the knee-high advertising board outside the shop opposite. Riots Latest. More Arrests. Last Karim had heard, the Asian lads who had been caught on the police's mobile CCTV van lobbing bricks were being picked up. They had not yet tracked down any of the white people. Karim was about to nip across the road and buy the paper when his mobile rang. He grinned: it was playing the Bollywood ringtone he'd just bought. He did a little jig, which made his father look up from his Daily Jang and tut. It was a text from Wasif:

Going on the Strip. Meet me 6pm. With car, *yaar*!

Karim replied with:
Bit cold 4 it 2day?
Straight back came the reply:
Plenty Gal Out There!

The Strip was what Wasif called the main Asian food shop road in Burnham, one of his many California-isms. It was where the young, gifted and gilded Asian folk of Burnham strolled and associated, even on a wet November. With a quick excuse, Karim took off from the shop.

Karim, your gloves! his dad called. But he was gone.

Karim had met Wasif at secondary school. They were both good at Art and wore their hair the same dragged-back, raked-through, close-crop way. Wasif wanted to be Britain's David Blaine. He said magic was all tricks but people wanted to believe, you could see it in their eyes, and all you did was give them the opportunity to believe. Eyes were Wasif's speciality. He had a hypnotic gaze. When he made eye contact people rarely looked away. And they believed his tricks. Mostly he did card tricks on the street like his hero.

With Wasif beside him, Karim's own dream of becoming major studio film producer no longer sounded far-fetched. Wasif would go through the steps he had to take to make the plan become a reality: *Get a digital video camera. Learn to use it. Make a showreel. Find an agent.* When Wasif broke it down and believed in him like that, he himself believed. 'If you can dream it, you can do it' was Wasif's favourite saying. He could make the office buildings of Burnham become the New York skyline, he could make a walk in a park a Hitchcock adventure. He could make you feel you were a millionaire even when you had only two pound coins in your pocket.

The wind gulled, flapped and swooped on the crowd at the bus stop, jettisoning hard, ice rain with each swoop that stabbed into Karim's face. The rain bleached the heavy concrete mass of the Burnham civic centre and the looming CarpetWorld and B&Q Warehouse sheds into the uniform grey sky. Inside the bus shelter were raucous homebound school kids, nattering biddies, zombie office workers, shivering shop assistants and the Aldi bag toting unemployed and refugees. The ice wind herded them, the dark circled them and the rain sodded them.

Bus stops were one of the few places all the cultures mixed. Asians, whites, refugees and blacks all came together in these tin and glass shacks to be let down equally by the fictitious schedules of AnyBus. An Equal Opportunities bus service: it let everyone down.

Karim thought again about a car. He could drive, his dad had taught him in his brother's car, and he'd passed his test first time. He just couldn't afford the insurance. He'd always assumed Pops would pay for it. And he would have done, until the fire. The damn fire.

Just then, he saw a figure walking through the rain, walking as if bathed in Californian sunshine: feet kicked out in an 'I own the sidewalk' stride, shoulders back, head up the better to display the mile wide collar of his shirt, a spring in his heel. One hand was stuffed lightly in a pocket, the other easy at his side. Karim stepped out of the bus shelter:

-Wasif!

Wasif's big grin came on, he swerved over and he gave Karim a pat on the back and a gentle handshake, which Karim held.

-Still good for tonight? said Wasif.
-Sure. What do I wear?

-The usual.

Wasif squeezed Karim's hand a little tighter, then let go. He ran his hand through his hair, then rubbed his hands together. He opened his hands.

Karim grinned. He'd magicked a coin into them.

-OK, gotta go, Wasif said, and he strolled off into the dark. - Laters! he called back with a wave.

By the time Karim was off the bus, snow was falling. He loved this town, this landscape, even if it didn't love him back. He looked at the snow carpet and his heart flipped with joy. Objectively, it was frozen wet stuff, guaranteed to turn to slush and floods soon as it melted. But right now, it was magic. It transformed everything: the ugly frogs of the derelict mills, the snug, dark terrace houses, the huge mansions in the hills, the farms up on the hills, the school playing fields, the smashed-up cars on churned-up verges, the slithery, up and down, twisting roads. This big tufted, spanking white 1000 x 10000 carpet of snow. Karim chased swirling flurries of snowflakes, kicked up snow with his shoes, caught a flake on his hand. He stood and watched them: fat flakes, larging it in the air, hang-gliding to their millions of mates on the frozen ground. Allah the Painter was giving everything a lick, making thousands of blinding bright surfaces of it all.

He reached the top of his street and slowed, bent his head. He was walking the white end. The first Asians to move in here were Indians, getting away from the lower class Pakistanis in the deprived areas. The Indians lowered the tone in the eyes of the whites. Then Pakistanis moved in, like themselves, lowering the tone in the eyes of the Indians. Then the Bangladeshis came and the Pakistanis thought the Bangladeshis lowered the tone and the Bangladeshis thought the Sudanese and

Albanians lowered the tone. The vibes showed up in the number of parking space wars that broke out and whose kids were not allowed to play with who else's. It puzzled Karim. Why was it like this now when years back when he was a kid they had all got on fine? He remembered going to his friend Anthony's party...

A December morning, almost Christmas. He was nine and a half. He looked out of his bedroom window, excited. He'd begged and begged and finally cried until, muttering curses under his breath, Dad had finally relented.

On the morning of the party, the house was quiet. Karim got up and looked out of his attic window. A great quilt of blue sky was embroidered with silk streaks of airplane vapour, and a big button moon. He could almost reach out and scoop it in his hand. Dad rose early for a Saturday and washed the car. It was a big, four-wheel drive that he was hiring to see if he wanted to buy it. Karim waited an eternity before he was allowed to climb into the passenger seat. Dad drove proudly in it to the Pear Tree Estate.

The houses were a storey lower than their own house, and all the same: doors all the same colour, gates the same, fencing all the same. There were dozens of cars scattered along the road that looked abandoned, though someone got in one and drove it off. There were little kids wandering the street without gloves or coats. Christmas lights shone everywhere, winking in windows, draped over roof tops, in gardens, over doors, and plastic Father Christmas figures, and plastic snowmen. The lights did all kinds of light patterns: meshes, waves, red-green-blue sequences. It was like a film.

They arrived at Anthony's. Dad chatted to

Anthony's dad, Anthony's mum came up and wrapped her arms around Karim – her smell was chocolate and margarine. Embarrassed at his mum, Anthony turned away and laughed. Dad looked back nervously as he got back into his hire car.

Inside Anthony's there were seven others: five friends from school, and two friends of Anthony's who lived locally. He had cake and red pop on a red table. His mum had them sing happy birthday to Anthony before she allowed them the cake and pop. Anthony blew out the ten candles on his birthday cake, then they gave him presents, most of them gave him a card with a five-pound note in it, Karim among them. Anthony's house was already criss-crossed with Christmas cards on strings. He put his birthday cards under a real Christmas tree that smelt like toilet freshener. The tree was in a plastic bucket with bricks to hold it up. They talked while his mum was there. When she left, they had a game of tag but the Christmas tree toppled over and his mum shooed the boys out to play football. That was when the best bit of the party happened, the bit that ended in the mad chase.

Anthony led his birthday gang to this piece of tarmac that was fenced off, but the fencing was all wrecked, in the middle of a grassed playing field the size of two football pitches. They got onto it and there was enough white paint left to tell the five-a-side pitch. A few little kids with a yappy little dog made way when the gang arrived. Karim was on Anthony's side. He wanted him to win because it was his birthday but he was rubbish at football and Karim had to play hard just to keep the scores in touch. The little Pear Tree Estate kids gathered again. They watched at first, then started chucking things. The gang chased after them. They came back with older kids. The two gangs lobbed stuff at each other, bricks, branches, cans, till finally there were too many of the local kids against them and Anthony's gang all ran back to Anthony's house, breathless and glowing.

His mum shouted at Anthony. His friends all laughed.

-Just wait, I know their mums! she cried. Then burst into tears. And for the first time they thought maybe it wasn't OK what happened. On the drive home, Karim's dad told Karim he couldn't go to Anthony's again. It was the best birthday party ever. Cake, football and a fight. It set the standard through the rest of primary school....

Karim kicked the snow off his shoes and entered the hallway. He shouted to his mum he was home the way she liked him to. The house smelt of Friday cooking. The carrot steam had only just reached the hallway so it was nowhere near to ready. He went straight up. He needed to change and get ready. If she hadn't cooked by five-thirty he wouldn't eat. There was no point trying to grab something from the fridge, better starve than get ear-bashed. He went to the bathroom and showered, shaved though he hardly needed to, then returned to his bedroom and opened his wardrobe. Downstairs he could hear his older brother and Dad, arguing. Every Friday evening it was like this with them. He listened as he arranged his clothes:

-I won't wait any longer, Shafiq said, his voice bridling with indignation.

-You sign the cheques now? Dad countered.

-Under five hundred.

-Is that not responsibility?

-With a turnover of five hundred thousand, profit at twenty-three per cent, before costs?

-Well? Dad said in Punjabi. He did not understand what Shafiq had said.

-It's chicken shit! How will I gain experience if you don't give me responsibility?

-First you must learn the job, Dad continued in Punjabi.

-Is eight years not enough?

-You've done well.

-And?

-You have to avoid doing mistakes.

-I never do mistakes. I don't do anything. I'm just a fucking driver.

-A mobile ambassador for the company.

-A driver!

-Some mistakes can kill you.

-Like when you under-insured the warehouse?

Dad swore. -Thieves. Thieves with briefcases, he exclaimed.

-Or a foolish, out of touch, miserly old peasant?

There was a beat. Then Shafiq continued, softer, but firmly, like he was in charge. So Dad had kept calm. Karim continued listening upstairs.

-Let us deal in fact and reason, said Shafiq.

Dad sighed. Shafiq meant, 'Let me hit you with some big words you won't understand'.

-My heart is old underlay, Dad said, sounding wounded. Every sentence was a sigh now. His father had sat down, Karim knew, and was holding his head in his hands. -A thousand heels have pounded it, and now it is crumbling, it won't stretch to hold more pain, it will snap, and then where will we all be?

-Facts! Shafiq rapped, like he was telling off a schoolboy.

-You will take over the business. Do you want? If you

don't want, I have two sons.

Why drag him into it?

-You want that knucklehead Karim to take over the business? Shafiq scoffed. He meant his lofty intellect soared over both the peasant ruminations of his father and the stupidities of his college-quitting younger brother.

-He has ideas, modern ideas, Dad said.

-Now you're making me laugh.

-I'll give you responsibility. Only the streets of business are full of thieves and trickery. When times go bad, rats flood the streets of commerce and you need all the experience in the world to repel them.

-The market is changing. We need to…

-You rush me to the grave.

-You're taking the business to the grave as it is. Let go a little, father*: Budyaa noo jawaan khaa jandai nai.*

'The young eat the old.' The expression brought a smile to Karim's lips. The poetry of it. Shafiq spoke beautiful Punjabi, English and Urdu, the proper, educated stuff. People stopped to listen, enrapt, when he quoted poets. He made everyone else sound uncouth and clumsy. Dad smiled too, at the phrase, despite himself. He tried to come back to Shafiq, but he had only his blunt old weapons against Shafiq's sword thrusts.

-I sold door to door when you were in nappies. I never ate lunch – no time – I walked the council estates bitten by dogs. Paki! ringing in my ears, doors slammed on my nose, walking home ten mile, fifteen mile, my feet two boiled chickens in the rain!

-This is nostalgia, not a business plan!

-Chop! Chop! Chop! Your tongue is mixer blades. You make an old man lonely.

It was two fools kicking around an empty plastic bag, Karim thought. The idea of Dad handing over the business reins to Shafiq was as absurd as the idea of Dad in Bermuda shorts sipping a pina colada. He would keep going till he dropped. Shafiq had simply deluded himself into thinking Dad was serious when he said he was going to walk away from underlay and roll ends. It was all Dad knew.

-A business not invested in, dies! Shafiq lectured.

Shafiq wanted the business to compete with the national chains like CarpetRite and CarpetLand, and wanted the family to borrow a shed-load of money to start the transformation. Dad wanted a slower expansion. Shafiq had probably met some grasping chancer at a warehouse this evening who had praised his plan as a work of genius and declared his father an idiot for not seeing it.

The ding-dong went on, the whining of Shafiq's voice countered by Dad's thick, low syrup. Dad's despairing monotone always met with resonant certainty by Shafiq. -Borrowing is against Islam, Dad said at one point, -Your mother would die of worry, he said at another. Each defence was weaker than the last, but he staggered on.

Why didn't they settle it once and for all with a boxing match, slug it out till one of them dropped instead of this verbal boxing? Karim began hearing it as a boxing match. Shafiq his brother, buzzing round the ring whipping out jabs as Dad plodded on, his face bloodied, throwing heavy slow haymaker punches that could never land. Shafiq's business school jargon snapped out in English, the words a foreign language within a foreign language to Dad. Punjabi swear-words from Dad blunt the cut of Shafiq's dictionary stuff, which his Dad admired even when he didn't understand, like a boxer with too much respect for his opponent. But Dad had his knock-out punch. Any moment Karim knew, Dad would feign angina, and Shafiq, out of shame, would relent. Dad only ever won by stopping fighting. Shafiq had no fancy shuffle that could dodge Dad's tears.

-My heart is old underlay... Dad repeated, cornered, his gloves up against the blows.

Karim heard the downstairs door creak wider. His mum had entered. -What is distressing you, my love? What has Karim done this time? Mum said, in Punjabi.

He wasn't even there!

-What is the matter with your father, Shafiq? she continued.

-He was telling me about his old times in the business.

-Oh, Papa, your foolish memories. Come rest your head on my lap. I remember. You used to carry a carpet on each shoulder up the blocks of flats. You wore out three pairs of shoes every month.

-What kind of sons have you brought me into the world? Dad moaned, -Oh Allah who knows all things. One rushes his own father to death, the other a delinquent good-for-nothing.

-I will pray for you at the mosque, said Shafiq piously. He attended regularly and always performed his *Jumuah*.

-I am his hall carpet. He wipes his feet on me every time he visits, Dad moaned on.

-You want tea?

-No, damn woman, can't you see I'm in pain? -There is no time for drinking tea. I must work if I want to leave anything to my sons.

By which Dad meant 'I am enjoying luxuriating in my sorrows, please pat my head some more.' Dad loved it when Mum fussed over him, but always said the opposite. Did all families have these rituals?

From his wardrobe Karim had selected his burgundy shirt with the silver trim collar. His mum had ironed it brilliantly. She knew it was his favourite shirt. Tonight was showbiz. He stood at the full-length mirror as he pulled it over his shoulders then buttoned it, trying not to crease it, getting the tucks right.

-Karim, what are you doing up there? Your dinner's ready! Mum called up to him.

-Coming, he replied, in English.

Mum drove Karim crazy. Her life was drudge: cooking, cleaning, ironing, washing, looking after children, sweeping, making tea, making beds. Maddeningly, she gloried in it. When the warehouse burnt down she liked how Dad had to work from home for weeks. She liked they couldn't afford to heat the house because it meant everyone snuggled up to her for warmth. When Dad bust his back hulking a roll of carpet up some winding staircase she loved having him marooned in bed where she could mop his brow, spoonfeed him dahl, deliver his four-times-a-day Cocodamol tablets. She smiled through every disaster.

Karim went downstairs. His little sister, Samira, looked up at him from the settee and smiled. He hadn't even known she was there. He smiled back at her, soothed.

-Out tonight? she asked.

He nodded. -You want chocolate?

-A Twix.

His younger sister was gobsmackingly beautiful. She had looked like a doll as a baby and still had the porcelain skin and elegance. He worried about her being married off. He had heard his mum nattering to his aunts that she thought sixteen to nineteen was the right age. -After that they can't be moulded, they're too set in their ways, she'd said, laughing. Samira was almost sixteen now. Did they have to let some slavering old cousin from Pakistan gets his paws on his little sister? The thought made Karim's head spin. Samira was popular. She could do better than that. She had lots of boys always phoning. Which was why she was locked in the house permanently after school.

This house of grunts and sobs and sighs. This house of smothered lives. It was driving him crazy. He had to get out.

-Hey, brother what's with the long face? Where d'you get that shirt? Shafiq said to him.

-Why?

-I want one.

-Don't take the piss.

-I'm serious. You're a fabulous dresser. Me? I have to wear this suit all the time because I'm no good at fashion. I look bad in everything. Don't I always say that you've got style coming out of every pore? Right, Karim?

Karim smiled -Yeah, he said to his brother, because it was true. And he looked up and loved and hated his older brother in the same moment and wondered how his brother did that, made him like him, even when he didn't want to.

-You think it would look good on me, then?

-Nah, stick to the suit, Karim said.

Samira laughed and Shafiq gave him a brotherly pat on the back.

Shafiq always took firm strides into the world. He

had got married, passed exams, set up an on-line fruit juice business. Everything he did he did well, as if he had the formula for life in his back pocket. Everybody showered praise on him. Everybody wanted him to visit them so they could bask in his success. If the two of them were in the room people hardly noticed Karim. He became like a hat stand. It was all: -Shafiq give me your coat, Shafiq what do you want to drink? Shafiq, sit here I have plumped up the cushion. Oh Karim, take Shafiq's scarf and hang it up. Yes, Karim, the cloak-room attendant. Even if his brother died they'd still all be at it: -Look what a good corpse Shafiq makes, see how he lies so neat and still in the casket. What a handsome star he'll be in Paradise.

Dad walked in. Karim saw Shafiq prickle. Quickly, he pressed home his advantage.

-I'm taking the car. Any objections? Karim said.

As expected, neither brother nor father replied, each intent on the other. Quickly Karim closed the living room door behind him. He fished his brother's car keys from the entrance hall table and took off. He had asked. Samira had heard and would be his witness tomorrow. Time to party.

2

Karim drove to the street corner where Wasif was waiting. Wasif was banned from calling at the house after he pranged Dad's last car. Wasif was dressed 'flash casual': sky blue silk shirt, close cut, black Chinos, patent black shoes, patent black buckle belt. Spiky, stir-fried hair. Karim had told him to lose the belt but Wasif insisted it was part of the image. -Check David Blaine, he wears a belt, he'd told him.

Wasif waved for Karim to get out of the car. They both stood on the snowed-under pavement. -Watch this, Wasif said, eagerly.

He made a ninety-degree turn away from Karim and tried the feet elevation trick, the David Blaine one that made you look like you were floating on air.

-Nah, I can see your back foot arched up, Karim pronounced.

-Shit. OK, OK. Let's practise. He produced a pack of cards. -Pick a card, any card.

-Surprise, it's the two of spades.

-Come on. Just pick.

The trick was the one where he had girls pick a card, put it back, he says 'Kazoom' and her card appears in the restaurant window. Wasif used a trick pack in which half of the pack was the two of spades and all two of spades were a quarter centimetre longer than the other cards so when he fanned them out they were the ones proffered. Karim had to sit at the restaurant window table pretending to have dinner and not know Wasif. Then, at the right moment, when Wasif went Kazoom! Karim stuck a two of spades up in the window. It cost in onion bhajis, that trick.

After Wasif had practised twice to his satisfaction, they drove on. The Strip was manic. The caterwaul of an ambulance fighting its way through and away briefly overpowered the buzz of voices and the rumble of cars braking, and engines starting, horns blaring, the crazy moped delivery riders, the amped-up car sound systems.

Shop-front neons scattered their multicoloured light along the road, and it washed along the pavements. Into that psychedelic streetscape charged the humming reds of car rear lights, the more intense reds of burning brake lights, the whites of plain headlights, the sharper tinted purple and blue of tungsten heads. All the parking bays were choca, even the bus stop zones were parked up with cars. People piled in everywhere, strolling, fooling, laughing, buying, selling. The fruit and vegetable shop fronts boxes cascaded to the edge of the pavement, hoardings were newly plastered for the Friday crowds with the latest Hollywood and Bollywood videos and big city party nights. Karim imagined it was like the streets of Lahore.

Later, he knew, the homeless would reclaim the bus stops' perforated metal benches and spread their blankets and top-zippered stripey clothes bags all around, but for now, bling bling shone out on the Strip, everywhere Karim looked.

Karim fought Wasif's Civic onto a side-street grass verge and parked up. They got out and walked. Nearing their spot, the two young men turned and paused. One of the shops close to their pitch had set up an outdoor cooking plate and was doing a brisk trade in barbecued corn on the cob, aloo tikka and chana dahl. People were double-parking their cars to buy. The heat and aroma blew down the street, tantalisingly close. They liked to work this particular spot – restaurant window close, and the Kulfi ice-cream parlour just a street ahead.

-You think they're gonna block our flow? Karim asked, motioning to the outdoor food stall.

-Nah, we'll get the crowd easy, watch.

Wasif launched into his act. He had no nerves, or if he had had any, the little puff of smoke he'd had in the car before they'd got out, had seen them off. He was flying now, Karim could see. Wasif planted his feet apart, tilted back his head and began:

-OK, *bundyo*, come closer for a bit of magic! It's a free show. Just gather round, my amazing powers will do the rest! He built his crowd skilfully, pulling off a few disappearing tricks for some white student blokes, then a few five-ring hoop stunts for an old black woman who offered to marry him if he could do it with money. He laughed that one off. The crowd gathered. He was warming up, doing the easy stuff, waiting for the right audience.

Nudge.

A group of three Asian girls were heading their way. They were in their late teens, totally pretty, in the latest fashion shalwar kameez, moving three abreast, arms linked along their side of the street, like three sisters. Already Wasif was smiling his big smile, making eye contact, waving to them to come over and join his crowd.

-Karim, the window!

Dutifully, Karim went into the restaurant. Three waiters converged on him. They loved the shows as much as the girls did. The window was soaking with condensation and he had a waiter clear it quickly with a squeegee. Timing was everything. He could see Wasif outside, carrying on with his patter. He sat at the window seat trying to look as innocent as possible. The three waiters all stood over him. It was hardly a natural scene. Who got served by three waiters at once? Karim saw Wasif slap his hands together, Karim's cue to be alert, then Wasif brandished the deck up to the sky as if summoning the power of Allah. Quickly, Karim slapped the two of spades into the window so it stuck, then, head down, studiously hacked at his bhaji. All three short-legged, white-jacketed, black bow-tied, moustachioed waiters carried on gawping right out the window, but the girls didn't notice. Karim heard their shrieks of delight through the glass as they saw his card.

He sauntered out to find Wasif with the three girls still there.

-OK. Keep hold of my hand. Look into my eyes, you have beautiful hazel eyes, and beautiful soft hands, and beautiful round br… earrings!

The three girls giggled and shied into the snorting crowd. Wasif kept hold of the prettiest girl's hands, - Where are you going? Good to joke. Now are you comfortable? All right, here goes. See this coin? Here it is. Now it's gone. Look behind your ear and, what a kissable ear lobe, here it is again!

He produced the coin.

There was spontaneous clapping that Wasif milked with a bow and a waft of his hand.

-Now you have to sit with me at the ice-cream parlour, all three of you, with my best friend, Karim here, and have ice-cream with me. I'll pay! He slipped his hands round two of the girls' waists and guided them and their friend to the parlour.

- Show's over, folks! he called to the rest of the crowd.

The waiters in the windows gawped, the old men at the shop tills frowned but had to smile. The girls themselves went his way, caught up in his style. Karim knew every five seconds in his imagination Wasif was undressing them, and that he got a boner from the feel of their skin through their shalwaars. The girls knew too, he bet, but he was charming with it.

Karim followed Wasif and the three girls and soon they were encamped in the ice-cream parlour. Wasif chatted to the girls like they had known one another for years, not minutes:

-And if they don't let you on that, do the HND in Art & Design, that's the easiest, plenty of free time.

-You think so, Wasif? his favoured girl said, gazing up at him.

-I know so. I'm in videos, but that's what I'd do. We're both good at design, right, Karim?

Karim nodded, embarrassed, as all three girls and Wasif looked over to him at once.

-He's quiet, yeah? Wasif's favourite girl asked him, kindly but curiously.

-That's because of your beauty. With ugly girls he's 'yak yak yak'. You're all so pretty he's lost his tongue. Why he's hardly touched his ice-cream – no tongue!

On cue, Karim opened his mouth and waggled his tongue, The girls tittered. Karim felt better. They had routines for everything, he and Wasif. He scooped more ice-cream to fill his mouth. They could hardly expect him to talk with his mouth full.

-Should I ring him? one of the favoured girl's friends asked.

-Let him ring you, Wasif advised.

-What if he doesn't?

-Then text him goodbye! Plenty more fish in the sea,

girl.

The three sisters loved him. He was part older brother, part randy young man, and part celebrity. One of them had placed her hand on his knee. He let it rest there for a minute but now he was playing with her, letting his fingers wander up her sleeve.

The girl squealed, but let him, till he tickled her lightly in the ribs and she fended him off. He had all the patter. Now infantile, now sexy, now serious, now joking; he was so at ease, so gracious. Karim watched and tried to memorise.

Finally Karim saw the girls all look at each other. It was just a momentary shared glance but he knew what it meant. All girls had these codes, a little flick of the eyelash could stand in for a thousand words. This one meant they had to be going. Wasif had read it too. He stood up off his stool and helped his favourite girl stand. He kissed two of his fingers and placed the fingers on her lips.

-Ring me, yeah? he said.

She nodded.

Then the three were gone into the neon night.

They did a few more shows together. The night was soon spent. Lights dimmed in restaurants. Owners rolled up in Audis and Mercedes for the night's takings, and to check footfall, and sort out menu rotations and staffing problems. A waiter, cigarette clamped in mouth, pulled the window shutters down on the Koh I Noor and lowered the door shutter so he had to duck to make it back in. Light taxi traffic floated along the roads. In the sky, the stars dimmed in a strange after-midnight mist. Neons flickered off. Mist gathered. The moon faded. Karim and Wasif walked to the side street, and jumped in the Civic. Karim was mellow, Wasif buzzing.

-Three phone numbers and the tricks, only two mistakes! We got to film it, get a video to Star and Zee. As he spoke, Wasif built a short spliff in his lap with the rest of their Afghani black and half a cigarette. He lit it, took a short toke then passed it to Karim. Karim drew the smoke deep into his lungs.

This night had been special. There were moments in his life when he was at peace. Life was those moments. He thought about his dad and Shafiq and their meaningless arguments, people squabbling their lives away.

-People don't live, like being alive, innit? Karim said, blowing out a fog of blue smoke.

-Yeah. Karim, hand me back that thing so's I can catch up with you.

Karim passed the spliff languidly.

-Man, you smoked it right down!

They laughed. Rain pattered down on the windscreen and roof and the car glass misted with the smoke and their body sweat. They were on a deserted side street, safe from the prying eyes of passing police vans on the main roads. Wasif flicked the radio on and it scanned straight to Asian Sound. Asian pop came on – a sweet girl singing about how her heart was bursting with love and her mascara running because of her tears.

-Natch. Shouldn't have bought cheap mascara! Wasif blurted, and they giggled hopelessly.

-I could live forever like this, Karim said.

-Like it's the perfect day, yeah? Wasif agreed.

-Yeah.

They watched rain hit the windscreen a while, mesmerised by its patterns and drumming.

-Sometimes I think this whole world is an illusion?

And we could all disappear in a puff of dry ice! Kazoom! Wasif said.

-'Ring me, yeah?' You said that cool.

-You like the line? You can have it.

-She was pretty. Will you ring her?

-Just another number. Karim, Karim, listen, listen.

-What?

-I got this idea, fucking brilliant idea, you'll love it!

-What?

-For the magic, right, we're gonna do the box trick, the one where they saw the body in half.

-You think?

-Yeah. Course, I'm gonna need a body.

-Loads of people could do that.

-I need the right body. Yours.

-Yeah, sure.

-Come on, buddy, there's no risk. I swear. Magicians have been doing it since before the Pharaohs. Later I'll get a scanty clad babe in kitten heels, but for now...

-OK, I'll do it, Karim relented.

-We're the business, right?

-What's kitten heels?

-Boots. Long black boots. Puss in boots. I got to get the box built first. Who d'you know who's good with wood? I could go Iqbal's, the undertaker guy. He'll have a spare box. Paint it silver. We can do a show right here on the street. Stop the crowds, stop the traffic, phone the TV people so they can film it. We'll be famous. I'll be on the 'Jonathan Ross Show'. Then a bit part in a movie. Then Bollywood. Hollywood. What's my shoe size in American?

It was hard to hold your own in a conversation with Wasif once he got excited. It was like riding a runaway horse – you hung in there, never knowing where you'd end up, but the thrill was the ride. His speech quickened and the ideas and everything tumbled out. You had to wait till he'd galloped it all off, then you could ask the simple thing like:

-Where are we heading?

-Hollywood!

-Like where now in this car are we heading? Like when I start the engine, is it left or right?

But in mid-flow, there was no stopping him. Karim wound his car seat back and half listened as Wasif poured out dreams, plans, schemes. They were double high: from the Afghani and from the street show. Karim had to admit Wasif had been brilliant. A couple of the restaurants had approached them to do private shows, someone else had wanted them at a wedding. He had plucked a price of a hundred quid out of the sky and the wedding guy had agreed there and then and given him address, date and phone number.

-I took three bookings for you today.

-For us. We're a team, right?

-Hundred quid.

-They pay up front?

-No. Should they?

-No more weed left after this then!

Wasif took out a fold of silver foil from inside shirt pocket. It was his special reserve. Pure grown Jamaican skunk, he claimed. -We kicked ass tonight, we deserve it, he said.

There was hardly enough left to fill a half joint. Wasif built it carefully, took a huge toke, making the end burn like a red rag, held the smoke in his lungs like he was a weightlifter holding a heavy bar above his head. He nodded for Karim to come closer and catch the blowback. Karim leant into Wasif, put his lips close, ready to inhale Wasif's blown-out smoke. Wasif held and held. Karim waited, his lips by Wasif's, their eyelashes almost rubbing, their foreheads close enough for him to feel the heat of Wasif's skin. He caught Wasif's eye. Limpid pupils dilated to fuck, the flecked brown irises rich and intense. A small wisp of blue smoke escaped Wasif's lips. Karim leaned in further, inhaled the wisp. Their lips brushed. A spark ran through Karim and he pressed his lips fully onto Wasif's, kept pressing. Wasif fell back into his seat, spluttering, Karim on top of him, blue smoke escaping everywhere. Then Wasif was laughing through his sputters.

-Karim boy – the – smoke's everywhere, he laughed. -We lost it!

-I love you, Karim blurted out.

-Huh?

-I'm in love with you, Wasif. I had to tell you, Karim said again. He felt pathetic saying it, but he wanted to say it, had wanted to say it for a long time.

Wasif was sat up and serious. -Did I hear you right? Did that just happen?

-I kissed you.

-You're a lousy kisser.

-I meant it. I think about you all the time, I get jealous when the girls are all over you.

-Come on, Karim, don't go intense on me.

-I'm in love with you.

-...It's just a phase.

-No, I always felt like this, from, well, always, you know?

-...But you fancy girls as well? Wasif said, sober and composed.

-Yeah.

-So, what's the problem? You got the best of both worlds. His voice was light, unconcerned. But Karim saw through it.

-Me and you. It's always gonna be there now, like an obstacle.

-Tell you what, once a month I'll let you kiss me. How's that?

-It's just a laugh to you.

-Hey, look, I didn't know, OK? But I'm cool about it.

Karim tried the handle of the car passenger door. Wasif leaned over, put a restraining hand on his thigh. -Where you going?

Karim shrugged. He knew if he spoke right now, he would cry. He was that fucked up.

-You don't need to shoot off. We're cool. Stay here and chill a bit, I'll phone for some more stuff, I got credit.

- I… I dunno. I just feel like walking.
-It's pissing down, man. Don't be daft.
-I need air.

-This car's got air-con. Wasif leaned forwards to switch it on. On the radio, the girl with the runny mascara had been replaced by a boy-girl duet, each dippily in love with the other.

-Let me go, please.

Wasif turned Karim's face with his hand so he had to look at him right in the eye.

-Don't do anything daft.

It was cruel to do this to him, Karim felt. Have him gaze in Wasif's eyes like this, after what had happened, what he'd said. He loved those eyes. Wasif knew he loved them and could not betray them.

-OK.

-Promise?
-Yeah.
-We been through shit together, right?
Karim sniffled. -Right.

The sheet read two burglaries, a street brawl, the crash, plus a rental car accident that had put Wasif in hospital.

-For me, don't do anything daft.
-Right.
-You're still Karim. You'll always be Karim, my buddy, my spar, right?
-Right, said Karim -What are you doing?
-I got to do this. Wasif had leaned over and was searching Karim's pockets. Karim smiled at being frisked, even as a tear escaped. He knew Wasif knew he'd cut his wrist one time. A school sports day. Karim told everyone he would win his race. Wasif ran alongside him on the last hundred metres. He won and for one long minute he was the winner, then he was disqualified for having had assistance. The whole school mocked him that afternoon. He spent eight minutes with a knife to his wrist behind the sports block. Mum told him his grandfather was always intense too. Karim imagined his grandfather squatting under a Pakistani sky, looking intense.

-I got to go, Karim blurted when Wasif finally finished the frisk. He twisted in his seat for the car door.
-Wait! Karim!... Fuck!

Karim jumped out of the car and into the rain.

3

Karim ran aimlessly. Faces flung themselves up onto the screen of his mind. His father's, congested, tortured, pleading: 'My son a Nancy boy? But he fits carpets, he's not a hairdresser! Karim, tell me this is not true!' Shafiq, in psychiatrist's white coat: 'Working in a small carpet shop brings this on. Shafiq's Discount Carpet Warehouse Open To The Public would cure his homosexuality.' His mum, her soft jowls shaking as she pinched his cheek: 'I should have fed him more chicken soup. I'll go down to the meat shop right away!' He ran and ran till his feet hurt and his head pounded. The street lights lit shadows all around him so it was as if he was racing two, three, four shadows. Finally, breathless, he turned into a side street and found refuge in an empty garage. The pain in his lungs kept his furies at bay. He knelt at the rear of the garage, watched a distant, red street light flicker on and off, and listened to the sounds of rain on the garage's asbestos sheet roof. A cat meowed in the dark, nudged forwards, approached him stiffly. Karim put out a hand. It brushed the side of its wet, grey head along his thigh, then, furling its tail round him, ducked under his calf and came round to begin brushing his thigh again. It had no collar. That's what we are, Karim thought, two strays, two souls in the dark. The affection of the cat made him want to cry again. He allowed it to nuzzle into him. It stepped into his lap, where it sat and purred.

He calmed. He was not gay. Maybe he just had not met the right girl. His thoughts drifted on as his breathing eased. He was nineteen and a virgin. Until he married, he should play around like Wasif. Perhaps he would find a girl who he could lust after. Asian boys had more leeway than the girls did, when it came to romancing, but still the boundaries were clear. There had to be no pregnancy, no scandal, nothing that would affect the family's honour. Izzat. Family honour. It was why you didn't get Asians on these TV confession shows blabbing their heart out. Honour. Why you were meant to be a doctor or a lawyer or a successful businessman. Izzat. Why a girl once she reached about fourteen couldn't be seen out on her own, and especially not with a lad. Izzat. Their parents always thought about things not as they were, but as they would play back in the village in Pakistan. Honour. Homosexuality was just not on. Honour: if they did away with it, everyone in his generation could breathe more easily.

Karim's phone rang. It was Wasif. Karim didn't have the energy to talk. He switched it to voicemail then waited. After a minute, he listened to Wasif's message:

-Karim, ha ha! It was a good laugh. Don't go hiding away from me. There's a party on at Imran's tomorrow. Let's go, yeah? Phone me. We'll do some tricks. I parked your car outside your house. Alright? Phone, yeah? Bye.

A tear wandered from his eye. He didn't deserve a friend like Wasif. All his family saw was a flashy, dangerous guy. But Wasif had his back, every time. Even now, in the pits of all this, when he'd kissed him on the smacker and said he loved him, he came through. How many people had a friend like that? It was why he loved him. Damn, he loved him.

The cat settled more deeply into his lap, nudged his hand for him to continue stroking it. Like Wasif said, Karim thought, he had the best of both worlds. In theory. The reality was something else, but he wanted to believe everything would work out and in that moment he did believe. *Burnham is New York.* He picked himself up off the damp garage floor, stroked the purring, grey-faced cat one last time and walked out into the street light.

The houses seemed to have sunk further into the hills, ducking from the scudding rain.

The car was outside the house as Wasif had said. He turned the house door key quietly as possible and let himself in.

Samira was waiting in the lounge. -They're in bed, she whispered. I told them you were staying at a friend's.

-Thanks, he whispered back.

-What happened?

He crumpled into the sofa beside her. -Nothing, he said.

She held him. His little sister, holding her big brother in her arms. He settled against her. They were like twins. He had been two and a half when she was born. On the day of her birth, he remembered Dad, a smile on his face as wide as Burnham, singing as he cooked. Karim had never seen him cook before or since:

-The new baby will be coming home soon, Karim, isn't that special?

-Da!

-That's right. I'm your Dadee!

Daddy scoops Karim up in his brawny arms, flings him against his hairy, sweaty chest, sweeps his hair with his garlicky fingers then begins cleaning his face and belly with kisses that vibrate through to his face bones. Karim gurgles. Daddy carries on:

-Yumyumyum. I could eat you! Kiss kiss kiss. Yumm

yumm yumm! Daddy eating Karim. And new baby soon. Daddy eat new baby too!

Karim hits him. He does not want Daddy to eat new baby. Daddy catches Karim's hand.

-Daddy only joking. Daddy won't eat new baby. There. There!

-Me eat Dada!

-Now you're make me laugh.

A piercing screech fills the kitchen.

-Daddy has to put you down.

Daddy knocks the screech box off the ceiling with the broom and stamps on it till it is dead. -Bad screech. Bad screech dead now, Karim. Why are you smiling? You like to see Daddy smashing things? Funny boy, Karim. Yumm yumm yumm.

And up he went again in Daddy's arms.

In Samira's early years she was always ill. Her eyes would weep a yellowish fluid and her body break out into rashes. She would be drowsy for days. The doctors could never figure out what was wrong. Viruses, asthma, eczema, allergy. Every new doctor brought a different diagnosis. Lying in her cot with nobody anywhere near her, she would suddenly break into a high-pitched scream as if night ghosts had started jabbing pins in her. Other times she would grumble for hours in a low, agonised complaint.

-Karim, why are you lying there, my sweet?

-If Daddy hears baby scream he'll eat her, Mummee.

Mummy laughs. -Who told you that, child?

-Daddy.

-Your father talks nonsense. He won't eat her. He loves her, Karim, dear. Now go to bed.

-Won't.

-Don't worry, Mummy says, stroking his forehead.

-Karim guarding Samira from the night ghosts.

-Daddy is not a night ghost.

-Night ghosts keep stabbing her.

-Karim, they have to stop reading you those fairy stories at nursery, they are full of nonsense. She's poorly with an infection. Now get to bed.

-Won't.

-Don't make me tell you, Karim, Mummy says, stroking my head.

-Won't.

Mummy gets up, smiling. -Alright, silly boy, lie there, I'll carry you out when you fall asleep.

-Won't.

She leaves.

Karim bites Samira's blanket tight between his teeth. Now Mummy can't carry him out even if he does fall asleep. But he's never ever going to fall…

Once, Samira went so floppy they phoned an ambulance. The whole house waited in fevered state for it to arrive. Daddy was in a corner of the sofa, his head turned down from everybody, rubbing away at his cheeks with his hands as if he was trying to wear the red skin away. He was kneading the bumps on his face like they were bubble wrap and he was trying to burst the bubbles five at a time with the palm of his hand. Mummy was picking the baby up, singing a few snatched lines of a lullaby in a squeaky voice: *Oh sweet baby swing with me*, prodding her and when the baby gave no response, handing her over to an auntie, then kneeling by the coffee table in frantic muttered praying. The aunties circling like witches, their voices hushed as they discussed if the baby would need a hat, shoes, how many nappies, the gripe water, the jumpsuits, the bottle feed. And Karim, in the middle of these circling adults, sat on the thick glass of the coffee table with the elephant legs, his arms folded in protest. The air was warm, wet and sour with baby sick, clogged with worries that the manic four-bladed ceiling fan didn't disperse; the fan that sent shadows spinning like mad ghosts around the room – it felt to Karim like a blur of circling evil above them. And Mummy said there were no ghosts. Look now!

-Mummee, don't let them take baby to the hospital!
-Baby's ill, baby has to go.
-They took Auntie Naseem's baby there and then it was dead!

Auntie Naseem began crying.

-Don't let them take her, Mummee! Don't let them! He pummelled his mother with desperate fists. The ghosts must have got to her. Daddy pulled him off and slapped him across the face. Daddy's ring cut his cheek and Karim was glad as he felt the blood dripping, mingling with his tears. His aunts took him away to the kitchen.

He refused to speak from the moment of the slap to the moment Samira returned, gurgling, pink skinned and podgy, from the hospital eight days later.

Now, he knew, as he lay across his grown up sister, they were working on her. They were sly like that. More and more, aunts and uncles and family friends had been popping in, babies in tow. The aunt would offer the baby up to Samira and eye how she reacted. Worse still for Karim, Samira didn't sense the plot. She took the babies up without complaint, rested them on her lap and the babies would soon be gurgling away contentedly, which got the women simpering:

-How well the baby takes to young Samira!
-I'm sure she can't wait to have a baby of her own!

-They'd be cousins, second cousins – wouldn't they?

-They grow out of baby clothes so fast – if she has a girl she can have all little Waris's, I've only just pushed out the after-birth and he needs a new size.

-So how are you feeling now, have you had the check-up at the doctors?

And off they would go into the world of gynaecology.

They were actively plotting to marry his sister off. It would be less cruel to take a pillow and stifle the life out of her. He loved Samira so much he ached, and would defend her against all of them.

He must have been tensing up.

-Relax, Samira was whispering to him, -You're safe now.

The next morning Karim woke up ill. His temperature soared. He sweated and thrashed in his bed. Crud wedged the corners of his eyes and his eyelids scraped his eyeballs when he blinked. His body ached for sleep. Ill, he dreamt grey CCTV images of Wasif speeding along the Strip, Wasif doing tricks with his BMW window rolled down, palming cards, making day into night, switching off all the Strip's neon lights so thousands of diners and staff looked up, puzzled, then bringing them all back on again; Wasif conjured three ghosts of himself and they all played the same card trick simultaneously. Then the real Wasif placed his arms wide and concertina'd the ghosts back into his one real self. He made the sun melt and people stood in the street to collect the drips in their hands, which tasted of wild honey. He dreamt he was locked in the shadows of the silver coffin prop. Beyond the painted pine there was the roar of their crowd. He could smell the previous occupant's dead body odour and his own fresh sweat.

Rain pattered on the coffin lid Wasif had just screwed shut with brass wing nuts. Wasif flashed the gleaming, stainless steel blades in the air. The crowd had hushed. There were three slits of light where the blades would penetrate.   -And now! Wasif cried dramatically. The first blade came through the box lid, slicing through his chest, before emerging on the other side. The second blade sliced through his groin. The third was a skewer that ran through his neck. With a flourish, Wasif withdrew all three blades. He opened up the silver coffin. Karim lay there in three sections. His legs stood up and jumped out of the coffin box. Then his torso climbed into place on top of his legs. One of his hands reached into the box and took his head by the hair and popped it onto his shoulders. He was whole again. He and Wasif took a bow. The crowd screamed delightedly.

He woke with a start, crying out. Seeing nothing but his room, Karim drifted slowly back to fevered sleep again. He saw his father at his shop, his back repaired, drinking pure ghee from a Khan Brothers foil carton to a swirling musical backdrop, then burping, patting his six-pack stomach and sauntering up to a carpet roll. He flipped the roll onto a finger, span it round the way a basketball player could spin a basketball, before walking jauntily to a customer's car and tossing it onto the car roof. His father did a little jump and click of his heels, then sauntered back to the shop to fill his face with ghee again. His hair was jet black, the pocks gone and he had a Karachi Bandit moustache that he was wiggling at the female co-star who was sat in his lap, stroking his cheek.

-Here, Karim, *mere beta*, drink.

It was his mother, nudging him. He was in bed. It was dark. She had brought him chicken soup in a mug. He waved it away. It was flu, they told him. His body poured with sweat, his limbs were stiff. Another day passed. His fever yo-yo'd. Samira entertained him by reading from newspapers. The reports got endlessly jumbled in the fever of his mind. Some Asian lads arrested after a fight with a kitchen factory. A lorry folding. The M56 blocked by a burning dog. Two old people going on honeymoon with a lost caravan to Rochdale. Finally she read him football pages, because he never followed football and it was easier on his mind.

He dreamt of Samira hiding under his bed as they searched everywhere for her to force her into her wedding dress. Samira stayed in the dust and insects under his wooden bed slats. Germs floated off his skin and he sent them to the door to stand guard. There they buzzed: malevolent, purple tinted, translucent guard microbes, filling every expansion and gap between door frame and door, ready to rush out and besiege any intruder.

-Don't come in, the bugs will swamp you to death!

-Open the sodding door, his brother Shafiq called, -You're delirious, Karim!

-You're a funny guy yourself, Karim replied. -Don't come in!

-I'm leaving paracetamol outside with a glass, Samira. Get him to take it.

Samira brought it in for him. -You need to get your temp down. She coaxed. He swallowed the tablets and slept.

Next morning Karim woke and his fever had disappeared. He was ravenous. He tottered downstairs and polished off three bowls of muesli. Samira and his mum laughed.

Samira told him Dad had been lifting carpets again and was glum, his spirits beaten down by shop visitors' incessant bargaining. The shop was a millstone. Samira had caught Dad sneaking away one evening in an ancient suit. He claimed he was heading to an Urdu poetry evening and when Samira had laughed he'd reprimanded her:

-We're peasants but we don't have to act like peasants. Poetry is culture.

He'd tried to sell carpets there. -You're a popular poet, very good poet. Many callers at your door. You'll need a hard-wearing carpet.

Any gathering: wedding, music evening, Dad was now selling carpets, even funerals: -Mature feet like yours need natural wool carpet, deep almost to your ankles. Ten per cent discount.

The way Samira told it was funny (she was a good mimic of Dad) but he could tell his dad was distressed. Karim got down to the shop and started lifting and measuring again.

The wood floor section, after a slow start because they had stocked the glue-to-fix boards and not the click fit, was more than holding its own with the carpets. Karim soon had his own oak desk and spike and till. His Dad enjoyed his company, needed him for the lifting and praised him for the great job he had done with the wood flooring. Still, for Karim, it was no longer where it was at. Wasif's bookings were rocketing and Karim was earning more with Wasif than at the shop. It was a tug of war between his Dad and Wasif that Wasif was winning. They were doing long weekends, sometimes four days away on birthdays, weddings, and charity fund-raisers. Wasif liked Karim about him. He could do most of the tricks on his own but when Karim had offered to ease off so Wasif could make more profit Wasif insisted, got upset even, and so the two of them kept on with the shows. The drives were getting longer as they drove to bookings in Leicester, Bradford, Newcastle and London. They talked about everything and nothing on these drives, as they motored up the M6, the M60, the M62 and the M1:

   -What are we, Karim?
   -Burnham Asians.
   -No, what are we?
   -Burnham Pakis?
   -Don't hate yourself like that.
   -It's a joke.
   -Some jokes aren't funny.
   -...Why does everyone hate us?
   -They don't. It's just paranoia. We're magicians, that what we are. You ever watched 'Pulp Fiction'?
   -Cool.

They spent the rest of the drive to Birmingham dissecting the film.

The millionaire's daughter's wedding was their third wedding reception of the month. It was to take place at the Royal Hotel in Newcastle.

The magicians took the stairs down from their hotel room to the thump and wail of banghra below. The Royal was a fading Merchant Ivory set. Lavish Victorian-style carpets going threadbare clothed the Royal's 'Gone With The Wind' staircase. Opulent, but worn, damask flock wallpaper hung on the sides. Two-ton chandeliers big enough to fill the entire roof space of Karim's carpet shop twinkled a dusty constellation above them. A female unicyclist was performing in the hotel foyer where there was a hunky, James Dean look-a-like receptionist. Twin medieval-costumed jugglers exchanged clubs dangerously at the doorway of the wedding reception. The banghra band knocked off, giving the band's lead singer time to cool his gold trousers.

The wedding guests were stuffed and dulled by the time Karim and Wasif were due to perform their magic act. Children ran between and under white-clothed tables, chasing balloons, flying multicoloured popper streamers. The adults stirred listlessly in their sumptuously upholstered broad chairs, casting about for their own entertainment.

-What's with the hang-dog look? Wasif whispered to Karim.

-Look at them.

-That's why we're booked, see? To pep it up. Watch.

Wasif strode forward to the centre of the room and in a playful, razzmatazz voice called out out:

-Gather round, ladies and gentlemen, for the wonder of Wasif, the world's greatest magician!

Only a few bratty kids came forward. Worse, the adults looked vaguely hostile.

-Tired? Understandable. Wasif continued, unfazed. - As a special favour to our well-fed guests, Wondrous Wasif will perform his wonders right by your table, so you can see his amazing act close up. Who wants to be first?

Wasif worked the room. Karim watched and assisted. Wasif did the upside-down glass of water trick; then the escape from handcuffs trick, which drew a burst of applause from the table he played it to. Wasif winked at him. He was warming them, winning the battle, table by table. He made ripped up paper reappear whole and drew gasps when he not only removed a guest's Rolex watch without him being aware, but made it reappear inside a blown-up balloon. The reception guests were now calling him to do their table, impatient to see his tricks.

At the next table the woman Wasif chose to work was painfully shy. Her quiet sari wrapped round her rotund figure, she averted her gaze the moment Wasif looked at her. Wasif took her hand nevertheless, and gently coaxed her soft, short fingers back so her palm was opened out. He raised her palm slowly, giving her time to steady her bangles with her other hand. Then he made a bird-like trill with his lips and looked up, as if seeking the exotic bird that might have called such a song. Suddenly, he pointed down at the woman's hand again. Her fingers were closed into the palm. When she opened them, she was as startled as the other guests at the table to find she was holding a small, blue speckled egg. Clapping broke out. Wasif bowed to the woman magnanimously, and took his leave.

The bride's father at the top table was a seriously wealthy fancy goods importer. He had warehouses in Southampton, Bristol, London and Singapore and homes in Hong Kong and Delhi as well as England. He wore a pressed white linen suit, with wide collars to the jacket and a discreet elasticated waistband to the trousers, a shimmering gold tie and large gold cufflinks on the cuffs of a pale-blue, tailored shirt. He was short, in his late fifties, wore black-framed oblong spectacles and had his heavyset face set in an expression of weary benevolence.

Emboldened by his successes with lesser tables, Wasif approached him. First, to great mirth and joking from his business associates and friends sharing his table, Wasif made him take his wallet out from his back pocket and open it up. He appeared to be carrying little cash, just two ten-pound notes. Wasif took the two notes into his hand, clapped, then opened up his hands again. The two tens had become three twentys.

-But how? the host called out, amazed and loving the limelight.

Wasif laughed. -Magic.

-But they were tens, and only two of them, now you've made three twentys. Amazing! He patted Wasif on the back. He was a good stooge.

Wasif laughed again. -You'd make a fortune if you could make your money double like that every day!

The table audience guffawed. This man already had a fortune, they all knew.

Wasif bowed briefly. All the host's business friends waved their wallets at him. Wasif declined smartly to groans, and withdrew.

They did a few more tricks, then the banghra band came back on and they were done for the evening.

-I've never seen that trick before, Karim said as they settled into a side room at the hotel and sipped orange.

-Been practising, innit.

-You lost twenty.

-Forty. But it's business costs. He'll get us loads more bookings, man like that, you watch.

Karim looked at his best friend with renewed admiration. Wasif was smarter than he'd ever be.

Karim had begun keeping a passworded diary in his PDA. He'd marked with a star the day he'd kissed Wasif. That night, after the Newcastle show, he had written: *Fisaw* (he never wrote Wasif. Instead he wrote it backwards: Fisaw) *amazing today. He does not need me. He completely won the crowd. Lay there snoring on the hotel settee. Wanted to k*** him again. The way his lips moved. How can someone so adorable and* *clever have such an ugly snore?*

The tricks got slicker, neater, more spectacular. They had obtained a genuine magician's box for the swords trick. They were booked up every weekend. Wasif bought Karim a digital video camera so he could film the tricks and make a compilation tape they could send out to TV stations. He began introducing him at shows as his 'cinematographer'. Wedding guests began to ask for their own copies of tapes. Karim bought a computer and video editing software and set it all up in the back room of his dad's carpet shop. It took all his time learning how to use it and still he made mistakes. The Workers Film Association had a five-day camera-handling course for £380. A month ago it would have been impossible. Now, his share of the show money meant he had it covered and he was just waiting for the course to start. Meanwhile, he spent all his day time trying to teach himself how to use the editing software.

His dad began carrying carpets again.

Karim read film scripts. He would read a script, imagine how he might shoot it, then get the video and see how his imagination compared with the real thing. Everyone thought he was mad. Wasif got hold of a multi-region DVD player for him so he could watch DVDs from around the world.

It was a lazy, languorous late Wednesday morning when Karim discovered the single piece of information he was sure would ruin his life completely. The house had been quiet. Mum was off on one of her indoor market expeditions to Flixham by bus; the older brother was out and about in the van talking to carpet manufacturers, Dad was at the shop with Karim, drumming his fingers on the table in two minds about chasing the flies. Karim begged off from the shop to collect a tape he had forgotten that morning. He reached home to an empty house. The radiators were still ticking as they contracted in the house hallway. The infernal cooing sound of pigeons sitting on the chimney came from the lounge fireplace. The heavy winter curtains were drawn back, leaving only the nets to filter the January daylight.

He thought he had left the tape on the lounge settee arm, right next to his empty cup of tea. His mother and her tidying-up mania again. She never put anything where you expected. He would have put the tape on his shelf by the window in his bedroom with the six others. That was too simple for his mother. He did not even bother to go up there and look. She would have tucked it away in some strange, cursed place, 'to keep it safe'.

He went to the kitchen and ransacked the drawers but there was nothing there other than the usual pathetic bric-a-brac. He shifted the settee and looked behind it, tipped it over and looked under it. Still nothing. The heavy, high lounge mirror rested on the middle of the mantelpiece, its top corners leaning back into the wall, secured by blobs of blu-tack. The gap between wall and mirror was where Mum often slid things. He prised the mirror away from its securing blu-tack and, holding it forwards carefully, he looked behind. Still no tape. But he saw something else. What was this? He picked the object up with his free hand. A fresh pack of wedding invitation cards. And as he picked the pack up, a recent photograph of Samira, smiling, that had been tucked behind the pack, fell free. His heart beating madly, Karim seized the evidence. The mirror teetered dangerously on his arm. This family disgusted him. His parents disgusted him. He couldn't believe what they had all been planning behind his back.

They were at the invitation card stage. He shoved the mirror back against the wall. It wobbled. He did not wait to see if it fell. Slamming the door behind him he ran in the road all the way from house to the shop.

There, he burst in and confronted his dad. He waved the wedding invitation pack in the air, tears in his eyes. Words tumbled out of his mouth between pants and curses: -How long did you think you could keep it from me, heh? You can't marry my sister, *my* sister like that, to some cousin back home who don't even read or write. Don't you know how things are there? She has to be free. They'll beat her, have her scrubbing floors all day, and doing kitchen work. She can't even cook, she's Westernised. And she wants SKY not slavery, not like Mum. We're a different generation and I won't allow it. I'm not standing for it. You'll have to kill me before I let you marry her away. And you can go rot in hell for all I care, you stupid old peasant, sneaking around my back. You disgust me. You're not my father!

It was a lack of breath rather than a shortage of further invective that made Karim pause. And for the first time since he entered the shop, he checked his father's face. He expected to see humiliation, anger and guilt. Instead his father was smiling. The stupid old man was smiling. Senility. The ghee had travelled up from his gut and finally overwhelmed his brain. Frustrated, Karim launched another broadside, hoping to blast through to the last working cells in his father's brain:

-You foolish ghee slurping, pillow headed cretin…

His father waved for him to stop, one hand fanning the air in surrender, his other hand clutching his belly. Karim watched, astonished. Was this a heart attack? No. His father had broken out into a rolling guffaw.

-You stupid sausage of a son. It's not Samira getting

married, it's Khadija! Khadija, your aunt's girl!
-Oh?
-'Oh'?
-Right. Well, I disagree. I disagree on principle.
Karim's father carried on laughing. -This old peasant hasn't sold your sister to slavery yet, you numbskull!
-I made a mistake.
-Your bloody maths was never good. Two and two making seven.
-I said I'm sorry.
-That tongue of yours could whip the devil.
-I'm not apologising again.
There was a discreet cough.
They both noticed the customer. A builder type with bits of plaster in his straw-coloured hair and zipped leather jacket and working boots. How long had he been there?
-So you prefer the Axminster? his father said calmly.
-That's right.
-My son, he, er, he's a little Italian. Fiery, you understand?
-Should meet my daughter. You'll deliver?
-Of course. Karim, make the arrangements.
-Right, Dad.
As he picked up the phone to dial a taxi, Karim looked out of the shop door. The sky was a great expanse of ice cold blue that spanned the horizon. He shivered. Dad and the customer were murmuring away, grinning. He had got it wrong on the wedding thing, big time. Dad would tell Mum, Mum would tell the aunts, the aunts would tell Samira, Samira would tell... before you knew it, even the folks in the village back home would know. He'd be the international village idiot.

Sure enough, that evening they had their fun. Dad told the story. Everyone sat there gawping, waiting to watch him eat humble pie. He would not give them the pleasure.

-This great mastermind, who imagines his sister is marrying Osama? Shafiq cackled.

-I treat all of you equal. I won't hear you insult him. He is not the fastest but he has other qualities, said Dad.

-This magician who magicks his sister's marriage from behind a mirror! continued Shafiq.

-I only put them there for safekeeping. I didn't want anything to spill on them, Mum chipped in.

-Alright, you've all had your fun! Karim shouted above them.

They cajoled him to come to the wedding. He refused. It was a mixture pf embarrassment and stubbornness and principle, the precise combination of which even he was not sure of, but he was sure he was not going. He finally settled on the thought that if he went to this wedding, with Khadija being almost the same age as Samira, he would be giving his implicit blessing to them arranging Samira's wedding.

-Karim, be reasonable! Dad tried.

-Reasonable? He can't even spell it! And this is the brains you want to put in charge of the business? Shafiq fired.

-Here's milk. Go lie down, said Mum, stroking my cheek. -He's only just recovered!

-These things should be discussed more openly, Samira said.

-He only just recovered, Mum pleaded again. But the blood was pumping in Dad's veins now and he couldn't leave it, even if he knew how.

-Samira will have to be married eventually, Karim,

that is life.

-It's my life, Samira blurted, -Not yours, not yours! Not yours! You can't marry me off without I agree to it. I should be the one doing the choosing!

Karim smiled, glad his sister was kicking off. She had sat composed throughout their mockery of him, but now they were about to discuss her marriage over her head, she'd attacked.

-Samira, you'll spill your milk, Mum said.

Dad grunted, always a bad sign. It meant he didn't comprehend what was going on any longer but he didn't like it. He'd often complained of these family arguments, that started off at one place and ended up at somewhere totally different.

-This is not your wedding, Samira. We discuss your wedding another time.

Samira had the wind in her sails now, it was a beautiful sight:

-Why not discuss it now? I don't want to get married. I want to see people first. I want to find out for myself.

-What is she talking about? Mum asked Shafiq quietly.

-She wants to have boyfriends, Shafiq replied.

-And if you don't let me see someone, maybe I'll turn into a lesbian!... Joke!

-What is a lesbian? Mum tried.

-She has a boyfriend? Dad exclaimed.

-Yes. I'm seeing someone already, Samira quipped. -Joke! She was enjoying herself now. But the subtlety of her wit was bypassing Dad.

-She's joking, Dad, Karim said, quickly.

-I'm not marrying till I'm 45. Then you can marry me off to who you like.

-Joke, I explained to Dad again.

It was too much for Dad.

-We are talking about Khadija's wedding. Karim, everybody will be there. You expect people to turn up at your own wedding? Dad sat down and began rubbing the pocks on his head. -We don't ask too much. We feed you, clothe you for eighteen years, bring you up properly, pay every bill, take you to the madrasah, parents evening, sports day, put the roof over your head,... I walk door to door in cold rain and broken shoes to buy baby food... and all we ask is you go to the wedding, not to bring shame upon your family!

Mum burst into tears. -Be a good boy. Don't make your father sad.

-You can be the official cinematographer, Samira said brightly.

-What's that? Shafiq quizzed.

-Like photographer but with video, Samira explained.

Karim stood up. -I will go. As the official cinematographer, he pronounced, and left the room head high, before they could see how much it hurt him to have conceded.

Upstairs lying on his bed, Karim spotted the missing videotape on the shelf. His mum must have put it back on the shelf. Shit. If he hadn't misjudged her, he wouldn't have looked behind the mirror, he wouldn't have found the invitation cards, he wouldn't have assumed the wedding was Samira's, everyone wouldn't have argued, Dad wouldn't be down there rubbing his forehead, Shafiq wouldn't be quietly cackling. Sometimes, you fuck things up big time, he said to himself.

He lay back on his bed, miserable. The wind was

bursting at the window panes, pushing droplets of rain onto the outside glass that tapped like Wasif throwing a handful of sand. There was the low zum zum of HGV engines on Burnham Road past the trees, and the less frequent growl of cars moving along the road outside their house. Then the sporadic, maddening pips of the smoke alarm on the landing ceiling that had started this morning. Its battery had failed. Dad had not yet got out the ladders for it. It would drive everyone crazy if he hadn't done it by tonight. Downstairs, the voices had lowered to skirmish level:

-Boyfriends are a serious matter, Samira, Shafiq sounded.

-So is 'East Enders', so can you shift your legs please?

-Are you sure you are just joking?

-Tell him, Dad.

-How did the visit to Norton's go? said Dad.

-They have surplus hotel grade going at below cost.

-See them tomorrow with the cheque book. Our credit's good there?

-I think so.

-Post date the cheque thirty days. Say it's cash flow.

The 'East Enders' volume jumped and now completely drowned out the musings of the two carpet moguls. Karim pushed a pillow over his face and folded it over both ears to block out the TV.

Was Samira joking or did she have a boyfriend? He had an inkling who it was if she had one. The boys phoning were often friends of the boy who phoned most often. Adalaat. From what he knew of him, Adalaat was cool. He was a gangly, clever kid, always rushing about, doing nineteen GCSEs and captain of his year's cricket team. Calling Samira to the phone when Adalaat rang, he'd seen her cover her face to hide a blush. She took the calls in the cellar, opening the cellar door and popping it closed again, then sitting on the steps there with the receiver. She had asked Mum passionately if they could get a cordless phone. Mum didn't know what the fuss was about. Samira hadn't dared ask Dad, he'd have guessed. Then there was this new homework club. No school ever had a homework club on a Friday. Monday to Thursday, yes. But Friday? When she came off the phone after one of her cellar chats she had a glow in her cheeks. He'd never realised it meant anything. He'd just thought it was how girls were, they loved phones and chatting. Karim lay on his bed thinking it over. If Adalaat was her boyfriend, he wouldn't tell. Samira always stuck up for him. The least he could do was keep her secret. Shafiq was the dangerous one. Quick to spot things. Funny, Karim thought, that Shafiq felt threatened by him. He had no interest in carpets. He was going to be a world famous cinematographer, not a flogger of five by four industrial blue cord. Karim suddenly felt nostalgic. He would miss this house when he was famous. The petty squabbles, the instantly recognisable smell of his mum's cooking. The in-your-face wallpaper. Even the smoke alarm bleeps. He would take photographs of here and hang them up all over his lakeside California villa to remind him. He dreamed on.

4

The day of the wedding zoomed up fast. Karim stayed up nights writing and rewriting a shooting schedule. He made a list ready for his visit on Wednesday to the wedding hotel. He needed to assess camera positions and angles, to take light readings and from that to discuss with hotel management the deployment of extra lighting or at least upgrading the bulbs in the hall for the staircase shots. He had sneaked in once when he had been passing and already knew he was going to ask for silver drapes to cover the patch of green wall in the lobby. Green clashed with the flesh tones and it was no easy job equalising such things at post-production stage.

When he visited, the manager saw him quickly. He was a gym-toned, quick-talking man in his mid twenties, with a smiling face, short black hair, a tailored cream shirt with yellow tie, top button discreetly open and gabardine black trousers with understated turn-ups that lapped his hand-stitched black brogues. He was wearing a continental cologne Karim did not recognise but which smelt class. He had perfect dentistry. He pumped Karim's hand and went on pumping even as he introduced himself. Karim winced. White people's handshakes differed so much from Asian ones. You had to adjust quickly.

-I'm Karim Amin, the wedding film director. I've produced a props list for you and I've come to make some assessments on the decor.

-We've done several Indian weddings, don't worry, the manager said.

-Great, but this is a Pakistani wedding.

-Rooms are booked, deposits have been paid on the glassware and cutlery. Everything's in order. And don't worry about dust, these bannisters will gleam! Keanu Reeves stayed here last month.

Karim couldn't help like his style. -Great, he answered.

-Is that your camera?

-It's a Panasonic MX 500 videocam. I need the green areas there, Karim pointed them out, -curtained off. They upset the colour balances.

-I can have a curtain thrown up on the day. We wouldn't want to upset your colour balances, would we?

-I'm thinking a ruched silver silk drape on a silver rail, to maximise the light.

-I'll see what I can do, Mr Amin.

-It's a lovely hotel.

-It'll be a lovely wedding. I like your shoes. Black and white checks. Nice.

-I work in the entertainment industry. You've got to razzle dazzle, right?

-Sure, kid.

Karim didn't like the 'kid', but he was big enough to let it go. -About the light fittings, can we walk around? These fittings at the landing, I'll be panning up and they'll need to...

Half an hour later the hotel manager clapped a hand on Karim's back and steered him past Reception towards the tall entrance doors of the Bedford Hotel.

-Well, here's your list, Karim said warmly, holding out his set of requests.

-We had a tattoo artists' convention here last week.

Karim did not know quite get the connection but he

thought the manager meant well, and after a mutually firm handshake left the hotel in an upbeat frame of mind. The manager had been attentive and had promised to do his best to meet the technical requirements. Karim knew what he himself had to do. A slow, ascending pan shot that took in the majesty of the ceiling and avoided the cracked mouldings, then a mid close-up on the couple's faces that pulled back to show their wedding clothes and jewellery, then, keeping them framed, holding till halfway down the staircase, he would zoom out smoothly to take in the full grandeur of the chandeliers, the sweep of the polished bannister and hopefully the confetti-tossing crowd below them. The confetti colours would be caught against the silver silk back drape. All in one shot. Satyajit Ray, eat your heart out, Karim thought. Acoustics-wise, he would have to rely on the videocam's built-in microphone, but at post-production he could mix in some appropriate music and fade that up at key moments. The logistics were nailed. The shots mapped. The sound sussed. Plan-wise, it was a wrap. Of course his uncle and other family amateurs would be filming the hotel entrance and some other minor shots like into and out of the car and arrival and vows. He was saving his expertise for the crucial scenes.

Was any wedding day ever any different? The morning of the big day came and Mum had forced Dad into a black suit two sizes too small and a white shirt with a newly stitched frothy frill at the front that disguised the straining buttons. -When did this suit shrink? Dad joked, and Mum cuddled him. Shafiq had got himself togged up in a black hire suit with wide, satin lapels and a kung fu sash that he'd wound round his stomach.

He'd also sloshed his hair with some mutant blue gel and shaved his chin so it stuck out like he'd swapped with Kirk Douglas.

-It's a cummerbund, not a kung fu sash! Shafiq had cried at him when Karim unleashed a flurry of karate chops at his brother's podgy midriff in the kitchen and skipped away. His brother was slower on his feet than Karim.

Mum had never looked so beautiful. Weddings always brought her out in a glow. She radiated joy in her weddings kameez. -Allah bless the happy couple! Allah bless the happy parents! Allah bless the happy family! she cried at regular intervals.

Karim understood her emotion, even if he didn't buy into it. A wedding was the triumph of hope over experience. He'd heard that line in an old movie. It sounded sophisticated.

Samira was stunning in a shimmering gold and red shalwar kameez. Her skin was translucent. Her figure had become so womanly you had to look twice, and the box-fresh pink strap shoes showed off the elegance of her ankles. Karim had to look away: she was painfully pretty. Even when she ran though the house shouting, -Who's got my fookin' hair dryer? I want it now!, everyone forgave the gob on her, so stunning did she look. Frankly, it disconcerted Karim. The witches would be marrying her off pronto.

They were hurrying him to get into the cars with them, but he didn't want to.

-Out! Out! I need quiet to memorise the storyboard! he shouted at a perplexed bunch of close and distant relatives. Kissing him, admonishing him, begging him to not waste time dawdling, but careful not to upset him in case he changed his mind again and said he was not coming, the wedding delegation herded into three top-of-the-range rental Mercedes to make their way to the hotel.

The door slammed. Finally peace, Karim thought. He was on his own. Wasif had a booking in Preston. He decided to go through his check list one last time. He slid the much folded and unfolded sheet of paper from his back pocket. It looked good, but the paper was no substitute for Wasif's calm promptings. He looked down the list. He was about to phone a taxi when a text message woke his mobile. From the first two notes of the ringtone he knew it was Wasif. What could he want?

Want a lift? Am outside yr house.

A lop-sided grin split Karim's face. He looked out. Wasif was here. He immediately felt calmer, and paradoxically, excited. He grabbed all his photography tackle, charged to the door and bundled into the blue Beamer. Wasif had the motor running and they swept off.

-Where'd you get this?

Wasif smiled enigmatically.

-You're in the red zone. You got enough petrol? Karim quizzed.

-Deep breaths, Karim, Wasif chided, -leave the driving to me. It's a rental.

-What happened to Preston?

-I was gonna miss my best mate shooting his first film?

-It's only a wedding.

-Nothing is only. Journey of a thousand steps begins with the first mile.

-What?

-Confucius.

-Who's he? A new hip hop MC?

-He's been around. You packed everything? Tripod? Charger?
-I think so.
-Sussed the layout?
-Course.
-Permission?
-Yes.

Wasif drove smoothly along the A-road to the Bedford Hotel and Karim sunk into his Beamer seat. Things were chill. He was travelling in style, his best mate beside him. It was like Wasif had sensed the importance to him of this wedding thing. Well, he had, after all, talked to him non-stop about it for the last three weeks. Karim had filmed weddings as part of their magic and entertainments service, but this was family. Ever since he'd agreed to film it, he'd felt like he was carrying around an elephant on his shoulders. With Wasif at his side, the weight lifted. He began in his mind to run through the scenes and shots. Bride and bridegrooom were the stars. But other family had to have supporting roles. He had to know who was who for that. He'd do a cameo of the parents on each side, bride and bridegroom, once the vows scene was done…

Twenty minutes later, they arrived at the Bedford Hotel. Smiling and shaking proffered hands, Wasif and Karim sped through the gilded throng at the hotel entrance, then moved through the lobby with equal professional ease.

It was almost a tribal reunion. Karim's photographer's eye took in instantly the shimmer, the shine, the jabber, the entire dazzling spectacle. If he got it right, the film would be spanking. He nudged Wasif to swerve round the butterheaded gleam of his father's head, else his family might buttonhole them.

The hotel had done him proud. The lights were good, the brass on the doors polished up and they had tacked up a silver drape. It was not ruched, there was no silver rail, but it had shimmer and he could work with it, Karim decided. And the lighting did seem brighter. The bannisters gleamed. He was happy.

The bride had not arrived, nor the bridegroom. The two friends unpacked, set up the tripod for the landing shots, then hung around. Karim watched. Samira was chaperoned by Mum wherever she went. No guy had a chance under Mum's gimlet eye. Who was the guy marrying his relative? he wondered. From what his Mum had told him, he was the second son of a struggling chemist; poor but educated, and would settle here in England, maybe even in Burnham.

Another absentee was the bride's father. A software engineer, he had planned the wedding down to the last sub-routine. He had called at the house once, briefly, and shown Karim a series of printed-out schedules that took in food check, room check, parking space allocations, bridegroom's arrival, bride's arrival, general seating arrangements, association time pre wedding, Mullah's arrival, vows, association time post wedding, eating times female, eating times male, dining seating arrangements, musical entertainment... The series was endless. Of course, now the day arrived, Karim realised, the human beings had stubbornly refused to perform with the reliability of an accounts package. Even the man's own daughter was late. Samira said he was right now in a cloakroom with a wet cloth over his eyes doped up on aspirin. Karim swept the room with his eyes for the bride's father.

After completing a thorough check of the camera positions, the two young men hung downstairs in the alcove behind Reception. Karim was making calculations on his camera settings while Wasif, keeping him company, idly turned card tricks. Every so often somebody they knew would encounter them, and lean with them on the mock Raj era wallpaper to make small talk. A succession of interlocutors tried starting up conversations but something in Karim's distracted manner, and the pile of heavy camera bags and tripod beside them made the newcomers move on.

As Wasif was deep in the middle of practising a trick that remained annoyingly unworkable, someone paused by them. More precisely, a young woman. Karim surveyed her. She would film well. Her face was photogenic, her figure shapely, she had an angular face, almost like those of the black and white Bollywood stars. Strange, and fascinating to see such a face in full living colour, he thought. She had wonderful eyes, so big you could get lost in them, framed by long eyelashes at the tip of perfectly smooth eyelids. The lips were inviting, pert rather than plump. They moved:

-It's a good wedding, yes?

-Weddings? The triumph of hope over experience, Karim tried casually.

She laughed. Karim saw she was puzzled and impressed in the same moment. -You haven't tried it yourself then, have you? she came back.

-What's the hurry? Who needs the worry? Karim shot.

Wasif, at his shoulder and overhearing, arched his eyebrow and winked at him, then went back to his card deck.

Karim smiled. Karim Amin: Film director, Philosopher, Witty Rhymster.

-You're funny, she said, I like you. Are you two

brothers?

Carefully, Karim took his Panasonic MX 500 out of its protective sleeve. It slipped smoothly into his left palm and he felt the comforting hug of the strap over the back of his left hand. It was like another arm or leg to him now. He flipped the viewfinder out and gazed through it to check the controls.

-Looks like the bride's dad at last, Wasif whispered to him, -heading straight towards us too.

-Keep him away! Karim muttered.

-Why? Wasif asked, hearing the note of rising panic in Karim's voice.

-Not only the battery's flat, innit?

Wasif stepped forwards. The bride's father had a look on his face that said he thought they might be gatecrashers, but was going to ask politely.

-Mr Mirza! said Wasif with an outstretched hand, -I'm Wasif and this is Karim, we are doing the wedding photography. Tell me, Mr Mirza, everything is so beautifully planned. Was it easy to arrange all this?

Mr Mirza was instantly placated. -Easy? he groaned, -nine months three days planning, nine months three days of sleepless nights and bills and phone calls...

And, having found a sympathetic ear, off Mr Mirza went, telling the story of his wedding agonies, guided gently by Wasif away from Karim and the non-functioning camera and into the hubbub of excited, expectant guests where he was soon swallowed up.

By the time Wasif returned to Karim, the cinematographer was in a deep funk.

-I've got the charger but there's no time... I must have left it on last night when I was practising. A tear rolled down Karim's face.

-Hey hey hey! said Wasif. -You bought a spare battery right, when you bought it?
-Yes.
-Where is it?
-I don't know.
-Where did I say to keep it?
-In your car.
-Where's my car?
-Out there.
-It's in the rental?
Wasif smiled as Karim caught up.
-Charged? Karim asked, suddenly hopeful.
-Fully. I'll go get it, right?
-I'll come with…
But Wasif had gone.

Karim spent an eternity hovering by the stairs, a scared smile on his face, ready to run from the bride's multi-scheduled father, before Wasif got back. He had the spare in his hand. Karim jammed it on the videocam and looked through the viewfinder. The power light came full on. He hugged Wasif till Wasif groaned.

-You did it, not me, Wasif whispered to him, as he let him go. -You were the one who said we had to have a spare just in case.

-Did the bride arrive yet?
-I didn't see her in the car park.
Karim filmed the wedding. He got all his shots.

Two hours later the wedding tape was safely stored in the boot of Wasif's car, together with all the camera equipment bar Karim's handheld Panasonic MX 500. Karim loaded a fresh tape and was filming nothing in particular. The entertainment and socialising had started.

He had almost forgotten about her. In the riot of

colour and swirling cloth it would have been difficult to pick her out. As before, she suddenly materialised beside him. The long thin neck, the warm terracotta skin tone enhanced by blusher, the long nose and glittering eyes. It was only gradually that he became aware it was the girl he had chatted to before. Now here she was, hovering an arm's length away: distant enough not to arouse any suspicion, yet close enough to talk.

-Hi again.

Suddenly Karim's tongue was dry. What should he say? The moment was passing. He knew girls. She would swing away, catch the eye of a friend and be gone. He cursed his inarticulacy.

-Do you come here often? Karim blurted.

She looked across at him with those eyes. -Only when there's a wedding. How about you?

-I'm the official photographer, he said uselessly. Now that he knew she was interested in him, he had lost all his former sophistication.

-Yes, I saw you walking backwards down the stairs, filming.

-Tricks of the trade, he said. -I can walk forwards too.

She laughed, and he laughed too, surprised by his own joke. Where had that come from? Her hair was jet black.

-Can you walk up the stairs? she said.

-Come again?

-It's a little crowded here. We can talk better.

-Of course.

-I'll follow you.

Karim began walking, conscious she was watching him as he moved. Did this happen to all boys his age? Was it a ritual he did not know about? He was dying to ask Wasif but Wasif was nowhere to be seen. This girl and him were definitely hot. This was him, Karim, not Wasif, not some dream or fantasy. He and the girl were about to, well, meet upstairs.

Suddenly walking was not as easy as he'd known. Each limb, whether arm or leg, had to receive the correct command in the correct sequence for it to happen, he realised. Anybody noticing might have thought Karim Amin's manner of walking at the time rather stiff and hesitant, as if it was not a lush Royal Wilton Crown Regent he was treading, but greased linoleum. But no-one was watching. The social entertainment was in full swing. The girl must have slipped away from her chaperone, Karim thought. He used the bannister to steady himself. It was polished as the management had promised, which made it slippy. His moist hand skidded along the wood. What do I do once upstairs? Should I stop, go back and find Wasif for advice? He sleepwalked up the stairs to the first floor landing. There he waited by the rear of the landing, leaning on the wallpaper as nonchalantly as he could manage. The girl with the terracotta face ascended. She had nice breasts, he couldn't help noticing, neatly wrapped and yet somehow straining to be freed. He arranged his pose, leaned back, like he had these clandestine meetings with girls all the time. At the top of the stairs the girl turned, saw him, smiled, then came towards him, stopping an arm's length away. She leant on the wall in an identical manner to himself.

-How are you feeling?

-Swell, Karim said. He tore his eyes away from the twin rises of her breasts.

-That's American, isn't it?

He nodded. -I just got back. New York, he heard himself say. Why are you making this stuff up? He made an effort to get back on track. -I'm Karim, and you are?

Shabina, of the beguiling eyes and sublime swellings, was easy to talk to. They swapped favourite TV programmes, most annoying music tracks, worst subjects at school and finally phone numbers. He complained. She said she would be missed. He complained again. She stepped into the gap, leaned down a little and kissed Karim quickly on the mouth. Then she walked away from him towards the stairs.

Karim watched her back, the sweep of her long black hair, the sway of her rear; and felt his groin stirring. She turned slightly, as in a profile shot, and waved to him. He waved back with one hand, his other discreetly wandering over the bulge in his trousers. When he found Wasif and told him, Wasif was as excited as himself.

-You pulled, mate. You got her phone number too!
-I can't believe.
-You hang out with an expert, you pick things up. 'The triumph of hope over experience.' That was a cool line. See what you've done? Wasif, King of Cool, is now borrowing your lines!
-What do I do next?
-You ring her, obviously.
-What if her family answers?
-Show me the number.

Karim scrambled in his pocket for the slip of paper. -Here.

Wasif glanced. -It's a mobile, innit? You're right in there. Direct to the princess.
-But what do I say?
-Just talk. Talk to her like you're talking to me.
-Like, in a panic?
-Like she's a friend.

A puzzled look settled on Karim's brow.
-It's not difficult. It's just practice. I'll be her. Come on, talk.
-Weddings. The triumph of hope over… Karim tried.
Wasif stopped him. -You done that one already. Comment on the atmosphere here.
-It's a wonderful hotel.
-I agree, Wasif said in an exaggerated, girly voice.
-Perfumes and petals and confetti.
-Yes, said Wasif dreamily, then switching into his own voice: Good. Very poetical.
-The triumph of organisation over chaos.
-Um. Profound.
-Quality carpets. Worn, but quality.
-Never mind the carpets, how about me? Tell me you like me, my clothes.
-That kameez you wore at the wedding, it was so...
-So what?
-Stunning.
-Thank you. Did you like it?
-I just said I did, didn't I?
-Don't start arguing, she wants another compliment, that's all.
-Your shoes, very nice.
-And my face?
-Just makes me want to... kiss you?
-Really? Wasif said.
-Yes. Like this.
Karim leaned across and planted a kiss smack centre on Wasif's lips.
-How are you going to do that if she's on the phone? Wasif chided gently.
-Dunno, but it was fun.
-You ring her, you arrange to meet her. At the ice-

cream place, yeah? And ask her to bring a friend: for me. We can show them our act, then do ice-cream.

-OK. I got it.

Karim was content. Wasif rarely let him kiss him, Karim thought. He had to take the chances when they arose. And when he did kiss him, it changed Karim's whole world. Suddenly all the obstacles and frustrations faded away. People spent too much time in pettiness. They should live the moment more. Nestling into the bannister rails, Karim panned across faces. There were one or two people looking discreetly back at them. Were they sniggering? What did he care, Karim thought. Friends kiss, not just lovers. It was their own minds that needed seeing to, if they suspected anything. He still had his camera in hand. He raised it, and through the viewfinder began to look for the mysterious girl in the red and gold kameez who had kissed him. Two kisses in one day. Both delicious. He wanted to record her. Crystallise her, in case, like Cinderella, she disappeared and he could never find her again. He was in love. Finally, he was in love. He loved Wasif of course, but to love someone of the opposite sex was new to him and exciting. He was in love twice over. Like Wasif had predicted all those weeks back, it was the best of both worlds. He imagined Wasif one side of him, the girl the other side, strolling and chatting along the Burnham Strip. Or rocking in Wasif's car. Heaven had many faces.

Karim's videocam roamed the gathering, picking out the poised but tired hotel catering staff, the tired but blissed older wedding revellers, the demure young girls in their shimmer and smiles, in which he had a new interest. He went from girl to girl, like picking flowers in a field, till finally he saw found the one, by the far corner, in a gaggle of similar-aged girls. He zoomed in. Through his viewfinder he saw elegance personified. She was taller than her friends, the slim neck giving her an Egyptian aura. She had a delicate way with her hands when she was talking. Amongst girls, she was a toucher, she always had a hand on one friend or another, and liked to rest her arm in the crook of another girl's. He would remember that when they went walking. Her hands were henna'd with an intricate pattern. He tilted the videocam up to her face and saw her looking directly at him, blushing, then covering her blush with a henna'd hand. Wasif nudged him.

-Don't blow it. Film someone else now.

Reluctantly he panned across, but nothing struck him as interesting compared to the girl in the red and gold kameez.

The calls to eat in the banquet hall came and went, the bride's father finally looked happy and Karim filmed him. He filmed his brother Shafiq and his dad arguing quietly in a corner, until Dad spotted the hotel manager crossing the floor. Dad waltzed through the wedding crowd nimbly as an ice skater through an Easter Day rink crowd, blocked the man's path with his body and a river-wide smile and was soon shaking the man's hand. He produced his gold block business card with a flourish, pointed to the threadbare Royal Wilton, pulled on his silver moustache, then whispered what Karim knew would be a price in the man's ear. -Just for you, Dad would be saying, -Just for you. The hotel manager freed his hand, and placed Dad's card in his shirt pocket. He nodded as Dad moved on to what would be his Taj Mahal comparisons. Finally the manager was walked back where he'd come from, with Dad at his shoulder steering, that sales gleam in his eye. He crossed right in front of Karim without noticing him. Good for Dad, Karim thought. Closing, even at a wedding. And Shafiq thought Dad didn't understand business. What Dad didn't know about the carpet-selling business you could weave on a two-foot loom. He filmed Samira, by Mum, with the smart-suited, sweet-breathing young males gadding around her. They had no chance while Mum was blocking. Karim smiled at their impotence. Samira saw him looking and waved him over. He waggled his videocam in acknowledgement. She did a little shimmy for the camera when Mum's back was turned. He laughed. She always made him laugh. What he would do if they married her off? The thought depressed him. He didn't even feel jealous when he saw Wasif had a huddle of pretty young things around him, and was doing card tricks without him. What he and Wasif had was something special that no-one else could share in.

This was it, as if Allah had written the script for his perfect day, and handed it to him as a present. He thanked Allah silently. He did one last round of the guests, not filming this time, but greeting and meeting. Then he wanted away. The day had been too perfect. He was scared something might happen to spoil it. He looked for Wasif. His best friend was still busy charming the girls. Wasif had been so good: remembering the spare battery, not complaining about the kiss, just being here on the day for him, when he could have been in Preston making money. He was not going to pull him away from his fun. Karim knew he had just enough money for a taxi.

The taxi driver set him off at the main junction for three pounds. The remaining distance was walkable. The rain didn't bother him. The blue and black sky was a glowering, Cecil B DeMille set.

He paid the taxi driver and ran through the rain, running for joy. He had a happy confusion of emotions called Wasif and Shabina. When he felt fragile, Wasif changed that to strength. Even about Shabina, Wasif had not been resentful. He didn't have a jealous bone in him. And anyway, Karim would never neglect Wasif for Shabina. It would be good, he thought, if Wasif showed a glimmer of jealousy. Had anything been at stake for Wasif when Karim told him he fancied the girl? Did Wasif actually love him enough to care? Sure, he was always there for him at important moments like today, but that was what best friends did for each other, wasn't it? Love was something completely different. Slowing from his trot into a walk, Karim resigned himself to the fact Wasif's feelings for him in no way matched his own love for Wasif. He consoled himself with the thought some love just is, and some love becomes. The longer they stayed friends the more close they would grow. It was the little things. Wasif never put his hand in his, but Karim would slip his hand in Wasif's occasionally then Wasif would hold it there, just for a moment. Wasif would put an arm around him when they were joking and laughing in company, but not when they were alone and serious. These subtle nuances, the light and shade of their relationship, Karim noticed, and Wasif, Karim guessed, did not. Whatever. And now Shabina. It was the first time he felt an urge for a girl. It meant he would escape the life of frustration and fear, of discovery and derision that was what being Asian, grown up and gay meant in Karim's mind. The only gay Asian men he knew were a drag queen on TV and a club night MC in Manchester whose mother was white so he hadn't actually been brought up Asian.

Karim's head was full of this and the beauty of the

sky which on impulse he filmed framed by the motorway flyover struts. His mind was full of the warmth of Shabina's lips as she kissed him on his cheek and her flowery scent when she drew near and how this contrasted as a different but equal pleasure with Wasif's hard lips and sharp cologne, when he decided to take a short cut along the narrow track that ran between a park of industrial units and some fenced-off marshland and that led to his road.

His feet made a scattering sound along the roughly tarmac'd track. Visibility was low due to the misty rain, the hugging shadow of the industrial unit buildings, and the absence of lamp-posts along the track.

Karim skidded on, unminding, wondering if perhaps he had been too unyielding in his total opposition to Samira being married off. The first noise he heard he took to be a rat bobbing through the marshland. The second noise was the sigh from his own lung as the knife sliced through him.

It was the last noise he heard.

II

5

The narrow roads of West Burnham, with their coat hanger turns and boxy speed humps were knocking four bells out of the exhaust on Delroy Johnson's Punto. He pulled round into the final side street and squeezed along two rows of nose-to-nose parked cars. He was scanning the house numbers. 26... 22... 20... 18. Got it.

He parked up on a grass verge opposite the address but left the engine running. The growl from the exhaust had sharpened after the last hump. Probably the front tube – a hole punched through its rust. He'd patch it later.

He killed the engine.

Number 18 was a tall, Edwardian mid-terrace in a solidly Asian working-class part of Freeham, West Burnham. It had white plastic windows and a narrow, paved front. Most of the fronts here were tarmac'd or concreted over for hard standing for cars. A quarter of the parked cars had taxi plates.

Observation was the poor man's credit check. Melt on the roofs and pigeons told him which of the roofs had insulation under. Number 18 did not, but its front outside wall had a caged central heating vent mid-way up that was pumping three sharp plumes of steam.

A grey-haired, squat, Asian woman in a plain wrap dress came out of 18. Carrying her head low, she took the two steps down, glanced right then left then opened a meter box in the house wall. A card appeared in her hand and she slotted it into the machine while her other hand held down a button on the machine. She glanced some more, right then left. Closing the box lid, she climbed the two steps again. Then closed the front door behind her.

Delroy snapped the poison-yellow steering wheel shield over the wheel – the shield was worth more than the car – then heaved out. A few nippers with no coats on buzzed around in the fronts, or else stood and stared openly at this burly, black man making for one of the gates on their row. Lunch was in the air, wafting from windows and open doors. Tumeric. Coriander. Chicken. He stifled his hunger. It was the worst thing, going on an assignment hungry, in an area full of cooks like this.

He whacked the muffled plastic knocker on 18's door down twice; a house as tall as this, you had to give it welly. A dark-clothed, big-shouldered figure appeared behind the scalloped twin panes of the plastic door. An eye went to the spy glass. There was the rotation of a Chubb seven lever, the withdrawing of a top bolt lock, the lifting off of a chain catch and the door opened half a foot.

-Good morning, it's Mr Johnson. We spoke on the phone? he said.
-Del Johnson?
-S'right, short for Delroy.
-You've come about… ?
-I'm sorry for your loss.
-I didn't know you were…
-Black? I sometimes forget myself.
-No, er, calling today. But come in.
-Better than when you're at the shop. I'll just take off my shoes, said Delroy. Shafiq Amin's own feet were bare.

They shook hands. Shafiq Amin had puffy eyes and

a trailing voice, but steady hands. He wore a neatly buttoned, evenly tucked black shirt. He was young enough to still believe everything had reasons, that a senseless killing couldn't be just that: senseless.

The narrow hallway had three doors off it. Shafiq Amin ushered him through the first door. He took in the room quickly. A newish beige leather sofa with its fire-proof tag still on, two matching chairs both with white doilies on the arm rests that would slip off if you touched them, bleached white net curtains behind drawn, heavy plum velour drapes. China ornaments gathered around the electric hearth fire and a bank of family photos in miscellaneous silver frames stood proudly on the MDF mantelpiece.

A teenage girl ghosted by in the hallway and he heard her climb the stairs.

The woman who had been feeding the meter came round the door with a tray and glanced at him. In her eyes despair outweighed hope fifty to one. She edged forwards with the tray of tea, sugar, milk, biscuits. The milk spilt as she tried to let go of the tray onto the smoked glass coffee table.

-Mum, her son started tenderly. But she was already gone.

Delroy waited. The older brother's face tightened.

-Excuse me?

-You're sitting where he sits, he said.

-Sorry. Delroy moved across the sofa. He knew not to disturb other people's ghosts, he spent enough time placating his own.

-Has there been much progress, Delroy asked, -with the police?

Shafiq Amin shrugged. -It's been seven weeks.

The door swung open again and an old man entered

in worn, red and white stripe pyjamas. He smelt as if he'd been roused from a five-day slumber. He stared at the visitor uncomprehendingly. His son murmured something in their language. The old man's eyes cleared a little. He stepped forward formally. -We are... most grateful, he began in English, taking both Delroy's hands in his. He stood gazing into Delroy's eyes a moment, with hurt and tenderness and bafflement. -I... we… he floundered. Tears welled. He let go of Delroy's hands, and, turning to his son, spoke in a torrent of his mother tongue, a furious, beautiful cascade, like tall waves breaking on rocks. He calmed, spoke in an analytical voice, still in the language. Then something triggered him again: *Police... Useless... Bakwaas... Racists… My heart is smashed.*

This last phrase he directed in English at Delroy.

The woman appeared in the middle of this. Now she led the man out of the room, his muttering echoed along the hallway. Who was he cursing? Allah? Injustice? The intruding light of the January day?

When he was gone, his son attempted an explanation: -He wants to go out himself and find who did it.

-It's pain, murmured Delroy, -he wants to lash out. He doesn't think the police are doing much, but he's worried about upsetting them. You need someone to look around, ask questions, but discreetly.

Shafiq was surprised. -You understand Punjabi?

-People. I understand people.

He cleared his throat. -How much do you charge?

The money question. He was never any good at answering it. -£10 an hour, or pay by results.

-Could you get a result in maybe, 10 hours?

He remembered the meter. -Anything's possible.

They shook hands on the deal.
-Can I look around?
-You think the killer's here? Shafiq snapped.

To lose a sibling was to lose part of the map of your life; to lose a younger brother was worse. An older brother always felt responsible for a younger sibling, no matter what. Their life's task drummed into them by their parents was always, 'Look after your little brother!' How many times would Shafiq Amin have heard that, Delroy thought, echoing in his ears, from the pram years on? And in this older brother's eyes, he'd failed.

-This way I don't have to disturb you again, he said.
-He had a bedroom?

Shafiq Amin's broad shoulders sagged as he yielded.

It was a box bedroom on the first floor. They stepped in. High ceiling, bed in centre, two channels of floor space to squeeze along either side of the bed. Stack stereo one side (with remote neatly placed on the CD player), bedside cabinet the other. An oak wardrobe by the door. Two posters: above the bed, Tupac, in standard bare-chested, tattooed, gangsta pose. On the wall by the wardrobe, in tight silver pants and satin bodice, Kareena Kapoor, young Bollywood film star. Kareena flashed more jewellery than Tupac, just. On the wall directly opposite the window, a series of small, vintage sepia prints of Asian film stars. Karim Amin had been a film buff. Maybe a media studies student, Delroy guessed. CDs were arranged alphabetically on a shelf, clothes in the wardrobe by colour. There was a scrubbed-up look to the room. The surviving brother hovered by the door. Delroy cast around, aware touching anything was tantamount to desecrating a shrine. A row of DVDs on a shelf, below that old videos. Below that some other kind of tapes. He picked one up.

-They're videocam tapes. He wanted to make films, Shafiq told him.

-You were saying on the phone, nodded Delroy.

The bedside cabinet draw held a deck of cards, door keys, a comb free of dirt and hairs. It was what wasn't here that bugged him. No diary, no PDA, no letters to a friend, no photo of a special girl. All those absences were fine. But there was one thing no kid Karim's age could live without.

-Where's his mobile phone?

-Downstairs.

-Was it on a contract?

-Pay as you go.

There would be no itemised bill. -Can I have a look? Shafiq Amin did not move.

-Has it been used since he died? Delroy carried on.

-Only if people ring, I answer, you know, let them know.

-Cool. Could you get it for me? he asked again.

-Now?

-If that's possible.

Delroy Johnson stood in the room listening to Shafiq's footsteps. When they started the second flight of stairs down, he sized up the wardrobe. Oak ones were hernia material. It was the only place he could see where the mother might not have reached. He put his weight to an outside edge and heaved, managing to turn it forty degrees. There was a thin sheet of dust behind it, spilling down from the skirting board. Then two magazines. He picked them up. They were both called Stud. And had pictures of naked men in provocative poses on the covers.

What to do? The family had had enough shocks, he

decided.

He was about to push them into his strap bag when he heard a polite cough. He turned. The daughter. She looked directly at the magazines in his hand then back at him. -Take them quickly, she said. Then added: -I knew.

He pushed the magazines into his bag. Shafiq Amin's footsteps declared his return journey. Delroy heaved the wardrobe back into place. He turned around. The sister was gone. Like an angel, he thought.

Karim Amin's phone was a silver, flip-up lozenge. It had a blue screen, picture messaging, a bunch of other icons and a snub fibre-optic aerial. This Karim kid dripped style. If the phone had had a security bar on it, his brother had broken it because it clicked straight through to Menu. The brother waited by the door.

-These things, they cram so many features, right? Delroy said.

He scrolled through Last Numbers then Address Book. Over one hundred and thirty numbers. -Can I take this, just a few minutes? I have a SIM card reader in my car.

-If it's only for a few minutes.

-Yeh, you can have it right back. Tell me again, what were your brother's movements that night?

When he returned to the house, he asked questions but found out nothing new from the Amin family.

Driving away, Delroy's stomach rumbled louder than the Punto's snagged exhaust. He wound down the driver's side window an inch, to help clear the screen mist. It was one of those snap cold days. Three dozen black birds whirled in a matrix in the cloud-white sky. People walked hunkered down in heavy coats and scarves. The backstreet bricks were iced. The Edwardian terraces pumping steam out of their steel-tipped chimneys. It was easy to imagine a hundred years back, how these streets might have looked. Same heavy coats, same narrow gauge roads, same frost and slither. And yes, it felt good to be doing this. Incongruous though that feeling was. He had more chance of dating supermodel Naomi Campbell than of getting a result in this case on the ten paid hours. But he was in with both feet. It was the heartstrings. He was a fool that way, didn't take much to twang them. Too, the police investigation was going the way these kind of cases did in Burnham.

He coasted the Punto onto the forecourt at the Denham Road SAVE petrol station and pulled it up on the pump, boot to boot with a Bentley. He got out, smiling and fiddled with his tank cap. The Bentley driver had that football star look, down to the Police sunglasses. Delroy made sure they bumped into each other as he started for his petrol pump nozzle and the driver went to replace his own. -Sorry. Hey, I'll hang that up for you, he said. -Don't I recognise you? Let me guess. You're a footballer?

The Bentley driver handed him the nozzle. -Hairdresser, the reality TV show.

Delroy put on his fool smile. -Damn, he confessed with a grin, -thought so, he said, -and you are so the best thing on that show. He let the guy bask in full-on adulation a moment. Then as the man turned for the queue at the pay station, he took the man's pump and pumped twelve free litres into his Punto before hitching the nozzle. He got back to his car and drove off.

6

The double glass doors swept back silently as Delroy Johnson walked into the infra-red field of Burnham Police Divisional HQ's main entrance sensor. Heat blowers activated, crisping his hair and drying his face. He trod the shiny rubber floor. The washed grey of the interior walls matched the mauled grey of the exterior. It was one of Burnham's few surviving prefabricated concrete municipal buildings. The others had been pulled down in the late '90s.

No one was at Reception. A motorised CCTV camera above the desk tilted. In the absence of seating, Delroy stood, dripping drops of icy rain onto the rubber floor, considering whether to go straight for the lift. He read off the floor list: LG. Finance. G. Logistics & Support Services. 1. Administration. 2. Intelligence & Research. Burnham Divisional HQ was not customer facing. Not even a bell. It was a training and intelligence gathering facility on the outskirts of Burnham. A place for public order formations, operations theorising, equipment testing and junketing.

Someone approached. Squeak squeak squeak squeak.

-Well, well, well, Delroy! You look like you've been hugging an iceberg!

Hilary Meadows. Funny how time warped things. The big bully in school now a skinny, shrivelled-up guy pushing paper in police back rooms. Lank hair about to go comb-over, squirrel eyes, the old flicker of fear and rub of the back of the head as he closed the gap between them, then the fake bonhomie. It was a powerful thing, bonhomie, coming from a guy in faint blue gabardines, a plaid V-neck pullover and rubber shoes that squeaked. Meadows held out his hand early for the handshake. There was a big gold band on his wedding finger. -Pissing down then?

-Clouds hanging there like a Renaissance painting.

-So! You're into art now?

-I know my Verrochio from my Michelangelo, Delroy said.

-Reminds me. There was a theft at the Gestener Gallery. I'll have to update you into the database.

-Do I look like a man who's got Picassos on my wall?

There was a beat. The two associates tracking the score. He needed Meadows.

-What do you do here then, Hilary?

They walked on, Meadows leading the way. *Squeak* -I'm heading up Targets & Statistical Intelligence.

-A desk job? Delroy heard himself sneering.

Squeak. -It pays. How much are you clearing?

- I get by.

-C'mon. How much? 15k?

-In a good year.

-And I'm on like 35 plus full pension.

They had reached the lift. Hilary Meadows turned smartly. *Squeak squeeeeeeeak.*

-New shoes? Delroy said. -Now you know why they put down carpet in shoe shops.

They got into the lift.

- I'll swap them in a few months. They won't quibble. A police warrant card works wonders on little people. Hilary Meadows' thin lips smiled at Delroy.

He guided Delroy along a corridor, the 'old friends reunited' smile flashing up on his face whenever any of his colleagues passed. They turned into a room with a couple of chairs, a desk, a filing cabinet. The door closed and Hilary Meadows dropped the pretence.

-I don't like you calling here, Delroy.

-You weren't answering my calls.

-Get a proper job. You're a grief freak, an ambulance chaser.

-Who happened to save your life.

Meadows groaned. -You can't live on that forever.

Delroy relaxed into his plastic chair. -Remember? You were beating up little Michael at the water park, right? And you went to kick him in the head and your back foot slipped and you fell off the pier?

-Someone pushed me.

-Down you went, screaming into the water.

-And that makes me your meal ticket for life?

-That's what your mum says.

-Leave my mother out of this.

-You couldn't swim. Flailing about, yelling, gurgling, yelling. All that crowd and nobody would dive in, but me.

Meadows shifted in his seat. -Alright, I'm eternally grateful, my mother's eternally grateful etcetera, but there are limits. It's only because you know where my mother lives. I don't want you calling round upsetting her.

-Do I do that? Delroy played with him.

-Like I say, last time.

-What did you get for me?

Hilary Meadows reached into the desk side drawer and pulled out a manila file. He pushed it across the table for Delroy to look at. -It stays on these premises.

-Who reported the crime?

-Some junkie who found the body and phoned it in. Victim died at the scene, of a severe haemorrhage. The weapon, likely a knife, was not found. We concluded it was a mugging. His wallet was taken.

Delroy looked at the murder scene photographs. Then went through them again. Karim was holding something in his open hand. The close-up showed a silver chain with a small silver cross on, the Catholic-style one with a thin, cloth-wrapped Jesus nailed to it. He pointed it out to Meadows.

-What's this here?

-We noticed it too. We logged it but kept it back, we didn't want to upset the family. We thought maybe he was converting. Can you blame him?

-How d'you mean?

-C'mon. Islam's a mad religion. Even you can see that?

-You read the Koran every Friday then, to make that judgement?

-Don't need to.

-That's cops for you.

-What?

-Nothing.

Delroy continued thumbing through the papers. -You've got a blood analysis, and a DNA report, Delroy said, surprised.

-Yes. Some of the blood wasn't the victim's. A match didn't show up on the database though. We're waiting for another similar mugging.

-That's the strategy – waiting?

-We'll catch who did it.

-What makes you so sure?

-We're bound to get a match in the end. Once these types do one, they get a taste and repeat. Statistics.

Delroy leaned back. -Well done on the blood, he said, and meant it. -But this strategy of waiting, well statistically, as you might put it, don't you think it funny that most black cases end up in the 'waiting' file?

-This is an Asian case. And we want the case cleared up as much as you. It's about efficiency, targets.

-It's about people's lives.

-Same difference.

-Black people's lives.

-We don't classify this as racially motivated.

-There's a surprise.

-Statistically...

-Fuck statistics, Hilary. He stood. -Statistically, I should've left you to drown.

Meadows, staying seated, smiled right up in Delroy's face.

-Sad thing is, Delroy, I'm a changed man, but you don't see it. OK, when we were kids I beat a few people up, but I'm settled now, married, two kids, on the pub quiz team. An all-round nice guy. Know why I got in those fights?

-Single parent family? Delroy sneered, -Mother didn't love you?

-I had Tourette's. It's a medical condition that meant I had a facial tic and sometimes I'd swear. It was a medical thing, out of my control. People didn't understand it then, even my own mother. It's gone now, Tourette's sometimes does after adolescence, but it got me into trouble back then. Fights, expulsion. All kinds of shit. It was a disability, but I'm changed, understand, I'm not the kid you knew, the man you see is not that kid, you follow?

Maybe he had him wrong all these years. There again, maybe he was lying. That would be more Meadows' style. It was a good story.

-How about you? Hilary asked him. -Got a place to

hang your hat?

-Don't get me started, Delroy muttered.

-I'm being civil.

-Well, you're treading on my balls.

Hilary Meadows chuckled, then rose from his seat. -I'll see you out. You didn't get any of these notes from me, remember?

They took the same corridors and the same lift, Hilary's shoes doing the same squeaks. They did another handshake at the infra-red doors. -Keep me informed, Meadows said.

-Yeah. I'll target who killed your statistic, Delroy said sourly.

-*You* don't change, do you, Delroy?

He drove away from the HQ hungry. He wanted to go home and eat. But Meadows had put his finger on it back there: where was his home? It wasn't Susan's. Susan had found out about Trudy and was threatening to throw his stuff out on the street. Meanwhile Trudy claimed she was pregnant by him and talked only finance and Mothercare World if he showed his face at her place. As for Violet, true, she had swung this office for him above the church and he had a pull-out sofa bed there, but he had to attend services as part of the deal, if he showed up. And it being Sunday, the chance of services was high. He drove on. To an outsider maybe it looked bad. Three women on the go. He was no Don Juan. He was just crap at relationships. He liked the early, flirty, phase. He was not keen on the His 'n' Her towels, and 'meet the family' phase. Could he change? Hilary Meadows, the bully with the peculiar grimace claimed he had changed. But the cynic in him choked on that. Maybe it had started as a disability, but maybe too Meadows the kid simply enjoyed beating up other kids. Plus, consistent with that, his Tourette's had finished after adolescence in his own words, yet he'd been a bastard all his later life too. If Meadows only knew who'd pushed him off the pier that day.

He drove on till he found a Co-op store and bought a Ginster's Cornish pasty, then pulled over and looked again at Karim's phone numbers.

Both 'Last Calls' and the 'Directory' function on Karim Amin's mobile phone showed a Wasif as the person Karim talked with most. Delroy rang him to arrange to meet up at a place of his choice. Wasif Aslam chose Jack's Snooker Hall.

7

It would have been better named Jack's Ghost Hall. Delroy squeezed past the unattended pay desk and took the dog-chewed steep stairs up. The Hall had blacked-out windows and was dense with cigarette smoke, and smelt of stale chip fat. The only lights were the harsh, low, snooker-table hood lights. There was a buzz from underpowered ceiling extractor fans and the clack of snooker balls colliding. Delroy's eyes adjusted. The place had few clients which was strange since Burnham college was only a hundred yards up the road. He made out six regional championship size tables in two rows in the far depths of shadows, and, nearer the stairs he'd just ascended, four American pool tables, all four unused. He walked towards the snooker end.

By the corner snooker table next to the shuttered-down bar and the toilets, a cluster of teenagers in hooded track tops that shielded bloodless white faces, were chilling, their hands tucked into their dark shell tracksuits which stopped short of glowing white ankle socks. Their gold neck chains and chunky bracelets glistened in the hood lights. They stopped their game, and struck poses, leaning on their cue sticks, cupping their chins with a hand, glaring as hard as they could as he moved towards them. Delroy paid no mind. Youth always struck poses.

Wasif and friend were playing with studied insouciance on the snooker table opposite the ghouls. He sized the two of them up. The player at the table had long arms, long legs, and smooth cue action. He wore a darted, plain white shirt tucked into the waist, a fancy belt, and dark, sharply pressed trousers. The glint at his wrist marked him as the first person Delroy had seen in cuff links in a Burnham snooker hall. His associate was younger, stockier and dressed in a plain denim jacket and creased, cotton beige trousers. He was leaning on his cue, glancing at the ghouls. He had a body builder's thick neck, squat legs and a shaved head. An opened plastic bottle of mineral water rested on one bank of their table, the water glimmering blue under the hood light.

-Wasif? Delroy said to them both, not knowing which.

The player at the table turned. The black, patent leather shine of his shoes was echoed in the gelled, black hair, cut short and swept back, and the black, heavy eyebrows that almost met in the middle. He had fast, confident eyes, manicured fingers. His eyes flicked involuntarily towards the ghouls. Wasif offered the lightest of handshakes.

-What's with them? Delroy asked.

-They're mates of Hubba's.

-Who's he?

-He runs the place. He don't like too many Asians in at one time.

-How many's too many?

-More than one, man.

-Asians includes blacks?

-No, Asians is Asians.

-And they think I'm Asian? He found it amusing for some reason.

-It's your bald head. They can't see no Afro hair. And you got no bling on you. Blacks meant to have bling, man, you know?

-We could take them now, his friend bristled. -We're three now.

-Let's just play snooker, Delroy said. -Do you mind?

-Go ahead, Wasif said.

Delroy played a simple shot and managed to hit a red. Not bad for someone who used to have the shakes. -Your play, he said to Wasif. -This a friend?

-Kamran. My cousin.

He shook Kamran's hand. His grip was one hundred and fifty five kilo clean and jerk, easy.

Wasif walked to the other side of the table to prepare his shot. Delroy went with him. -Can we lose Kamran for a minute? Delroy murmured.

Wasif waved his cousin over, talked briefly to him in another language. His cousin nodded and shuffled reluctantly away towards the American pool tables, giving a long backward glare at the Hubba crew as he went.

Wasif hit the white ball up the table. It hit a red which rolled neatly beside the top right jaw and toppled in. His next shot pushed the green close to a middle pocket. He and Delroy were side by side. There was a silence between them.

-How do you feel about it all? Delroy asked.

Wasif shook his head, his lips pursed.

-It's my fault.

-Why's that?

-If I'd given him a lift...

-I spoke to the taxi driver. He asked to be put down early, he wanted to walk.

-But if…

Delroy put an arm on his shoulder. -It's who stabbed him's fault, not yours.

Wasif seemed unconvinced, moved away from

Delroy and surveyed the table.

-His family didn't let me go to the funeral, he said.

Delroy played a glancing shot into the triangle of reds, bringing the cue ball back up the table. -Why's that?

-I have a reputation, you know? 'Wide boy. Stay clear.'

-You were Karim's best friend. They can't change that.

-But Karim's dead! Wasif Aslam whacked the white cue ball. It smashed into a triangle of reds, scattering them, holing two.

-C'mon, you can't blame yourself.

-Play your shot, man. I'll be right there. He dragged his shirt cuff over his face scratching his face with the cuff link.

Delroy went to the table, and sized up the angles. He could just about squeeze a red into a pocket. He took his time. Out of his peripheral vision he saw Wasif rise and come over. He hit the red but failed to pot it.

-Nine times out of ten I make that shot, he said to Wasif.

Wasif smiled tentatively.

-I understand you had a magic act together? Delroy said.

-Yep. Wasif picked a red off the table. -See this? He cupped the red ball in his hand. -Now watch. He threw his hands in the air. When they came down, the cue ball was gone.

-Damn. Where'd it go? Delroy asked in genuine wonder.

Wasif smiled like smiling hurt. -It would have been Karim who showed it you, he said. Reluctantly, he produced the red ball from his trouser pocket. -Now you see it, now you don't, he said. -Same as Karim. Now you see him. Now you don't.

-I'll find who did it, Delroy said, softly.

-Sure, Wasif said.

Maybe he had heard it before from the police. Maybe it didn't matter to him, didn't change the fact his best friend was dead.

They sat down.

Delroy waited.

-That night, Wasif said, -I had a booking in Preston, but I went to the wedding for him, instead. Not that he needed help, he was a genius with a videocam. Like an extension of his arm it was, man.

-Do you have it?

Wasif shook his head in a negative, remembering. -He never trusted me with it. He left the wedding tape with me, then reloaded. That's Karim for you.

There was nothing in the police files about a missing video camera. Delroy made a mental note. -Listen, there's something else.

-What's that?

-It's difficult to say it.

-Well, say it or don't.

-I found copies of a magazine hidden in his room. Called Stud.

-And?

They were talking in whispers.

-It's a gay porn magazine, Delroy said.

-And?

-You knew then?

-He was my best friend, I'm gonna know, right?

-Were you two...?

Wasif straightened. He tapped the cue tip on the side of the snooker table, making a mark where blue chalk came off the tip. -I loved him, but not like that. And he wasn't gay, he was bisexual.

Again Delroy waited. Sometimes not talking was more effective, it allowed people to think about things and choose their words.

-I was the only person he told, Wasif said slowly. -It's not something he wanted spread about, understand? There were equal doses of decency and threat in Wasif's voice.

-Of course, Delroy replied.

-Anyway, what's it got to do with anything? He was happier than I'd ever saw him that night. It was no 'gay suicide' or owt like that.

-Something else I have to ask.

-Go ahead.

-Was Karim a Christian?

Delroy knew it might seem an odd question.

There was a touch of exasperation in Wasif voice as he replied:

-He was a Muslim, like all of us, innit?

-Did he ever talk about Christianity?

-Never.

-Ever see him carrying a Bible, wearing a necklace with a Saint Christopher cross, anything like that?

- I told you, he was a Muslim, non-practising. You trying to make this some kind of religious thing, man? He's dead, someone stabbed him and took his wallet. Simple!

-That's what the police say?

-Right.

-What kind of video camera was it?

-Was the dope, man, a Panasonic MX 500, straight out of the box.

-Alright. Delroy put his hand on Wasif's shoulder.

He felt him tense, then relax almost to a slump. -Listen, hang in there. You're a good friend.

-Yeah, right. Was.

Delroy stood up. -Anything come up, I'll let you know, OK?

There was the merest flicker of appreciation from Wasif.

Delroy walked away, nodding to Wasif's cousin as he went past him. The cousin looked like he was itching to get a fight on with the ghouls. Delroy had other battles.

He drove two complete revolutions of Burnham's Prince's Way roundabout, unsure which exit to take. 'Like an extension of his arm' Wasif had said. Where was that video camera now? Karim had come from a wedding. He'd filmed it and he'd taken the camera with him.

He entered his third revolution. He meant to go home, eat, rest. But he was back at the same question as before. Susan and an ear-bashing? Or Trudy and her cot and finance chats? Or his makeshift office above the church with the fold-out sofa bed, and churchwoman Violet?

As his luck would have it, he arrived bang in the middle of a service and was corralled by Violet into the congregation benches before he could make the stairs. At least she allowed him to hang at the back of the pews.

He was never great at concentrating in church and his mind wandered. The Burnham Church of God of Prophecy had been erected in 1895 he had read on a proud plaque on the common-brick side wall of the building. The plaque pronounced the building a

Wesleyan place of worship for the God-fearing poor folk of Burnham. The church had been adopted by Ukrainian Catholics in the early 1950s when presumably Wesleyanism had died down, and, when the Ukrainians in turn moved on, the freehold was purchased by the current West Indian occupants.

This was how it was, how it was meant to be. Things slid into each other. Generation slid into generation. Community into community. Time into time.

The poor English mill workers became the poor East European immigrants, became the poor West Indians. In this high ceiling-ed, damp-trickled, ancient wood beamed, slate-capped, working-class cathedral, different congregations had boomed out their hopes, roused their spirits and shored up their belief in the better life: in Heaven, if not in Burnham.

The choir got noisy, died down. He listened in. The preacher was at the pulpit, taking them through a passage of the New Testament, something about the Pharisees. He began sedately, then moved swiftly and abruptly to a rapture, sweating up in the pulpit despite the draughts and the inconsequential blow heater at his feet. The mortar and wall ties were weak, but the spirit and the congregation was strong, Delroy thought. In their chorused whooping and shouting, if you closed your eyes you could be at an African ceremony of worship for a deity. But these devout and orthodox Christians would disown any association with African Gods, cast him out as a heathen for even mentioning it.

A song started up. He half-sang along. He knew many of the songs from Sunday School. This one was popular at funerals: mournful, slow, and steady paced:

Deep river, my home is over Jordan;

Deep river Lord, I want to cross over into camp ground.

*Oh don't you want to go
To that Gospel peace
To that promised land
Where all is peace...*

He drifted off again, in the middle of the song. *My home is over Jordan.* Home was always elsewhere, once you uprooted from the land of your birth. And for this congregation, without the means or the will to make the return journey, home became the destination of their spirit rather than their suitcases. This church was their waiting room. And though the sinews were slackened, the eyeballs clouded, their spirit and their vision was strong.

He looked around, counting heads. The sisters outnumbered the brothers by five to one. It was only half explained by the men staying away from church. The sisters lived longer too. They came to church and poured out their troubles. You could get a year's full of gossip in one morning if you knelt next to the right sister when the individual praying started. He remembered one instance:

'Lord, help my son who is seeing that nasty, foul-mouthed daughter of the Wicks. May he see the light of her evil, scheming nature, may he realise that she is nowhere not good enough for him. Lord help also my eldest daughter who is thinking of buying a house in an unsuitable area and far far away from her loving mother who would not be able to visit her every day at that distance despite she will need me once she has borned the granddaughter she promised me... And Lord help the man next door with his new drill who keeps me awake with his drilling and especially the fallen women who stay over at his house, the blonde one, she catches the 46 bus. Lord if you want me to find more out about her give me a sign... And Mildred had only twenty-three people at her funeral service and promise me, Lord, you won't shame me like that.'

There was a change of song. The saints were going marching in. *Oh when the saints go marching in... !* This army of Jesus sang with joyous abandon, close to the door now, on Heaven's doorstep. The choir stretched and danced and stamped. The building shook. The preacher flailed and, eyes closed tight, his face in a grimace of divine concentration, his whole body shook. His bass singing voice rang out, the congregation soaring with him.

Oh when the saints go marching in... !

Delroy found himself singing, even swaying. The church boosted the soul, even if you were a struggling believer like himself. They were rolling. An aura of hope lit up the church. Every face he looked at, in that moment, was in rapture, transported to a higher plane. This communal spirit, agitated and aroused by the singing, woke something in them, and drew something down among them from above, he believed, and stirred something from within for the old folks: past childhoods of driftwood and spring water, perfumes and calypsos, their first romances, the friends still back home and waiting; Delroy believed, really believed, it all came stomping back into this church, into this space and time, became true, real again, if only briefly, if only for the duration of their singing ecstasy. No-one with a soul could be unmoved.

And did he only imagine or did he see the Edwardian

poor mingle with this old West Indian congregation, sit among the pews, and the Wesleyans and the Ukrainians and the Polish? Were these ghosts, the imaginings of a tired mind and a hungry belly, or the conjuring power of religion?

Things slid into each other. Generation slid into generation. Community into community. Time slid into time.

After the service, Violet gave him a pat of encouragement. -It wasn't so bad, was it? she said. She played with a stray cotton thread that hung on his fraying jacket lapel.

-Some good tunes, he admitted.

-Admit the spirit moved you, Mr Johnson.

Violet did not look a day over forty. Which meant she could be anything up to sixty-five. He admired again her fine china features: the clearness of her complexion, the quirky dark spots on her left cheek, the ruffled flamboyance of white church blouse, the smart contours of the plain black dress that ended just below the knee.

-Lift up your head, Mr Johnson!

-Just a silent prayer, sister.

-And I'll take no more excuses for you not sharing a repast with me, young man.

He smiled. She was a practised flatterer and did the 'young man' bit perfectly. As for 'repast', she always spoke Bible when she was in church company. He knew her plan to save his soul involved a Bordeaux lace tablecloth meal for two at her place, with red wine in goblets and 'Sweet Honey on The Rocks' playing low. He could see himself eating her snapper fish and rice, then warming her bed. It would be divine, breathing the scent of her, close to him. But he knew if he ate that cake it would mean church services four times a week, and that took a man more devout than himself. That was avoidance, the little joke he told himself. Besides, if people got to know him too much, then they got to know about his stuff and he didn't like making himself vulnerable like that, it felt too raw. Nobody really knew him as it stood. He triangulated things. Kept everyone at a certain distance.

The preacher buttonholed Violet and he took his chance and left. He bought a microwave burger at a service station, ate it standing right there on the forecourt, then drove on. He could visit the scene while there was still daylight, retrace Karim Amin's last steps.

8

The scene was on the outskirts of West Burnham.

He parked up in a side street then walked up a narrow road with terraced houses either side, the type without any front gardens so they began right at the edge of the pavement, and you walked past people's lives if you turned your head to look in the windows as you went past. At the end was a short alleyway, and then the track. He did not expect to find anything that was not in the photos, given the lapse of time since the murder was committed. Rain, dogs and kids would have carried away any remaining evidence. It was more so he had a first-hand three-dimensional grasp of the geography involved.

The killer could only have come from one of two directions onto the track. The marsh land on one side was fenced off with eight-foot high steel spike fencing that had no bulges, gaps or breaks; and the same make of spike fencing corralled the other side, with a high, windowless, yellow engineering brick wall of a unit on an industrial park a short way back from that.

There was a CCTV camera high on the unit wall, overlooking the track. He would have to drive all the way round to check the CCTV out, a good fifteen-minute detour. There was nothing more for him here. He was still peckish but glad he had snacked on the burger at the garage.

New-build industrial parks were rare in Burnham. Land agents' books were brimming with Victorian and Edwardian mill space to flog. The brick behemoths that had once steamed and blasted Burnham to a dizzy position in the league table of English wealth-producing counties, were now mostly silent, hollowed-out testimonies to the fickleness of Empire trade. Unemployment started its rising curve with the mills' decline and, some hundred years later, it dawned on the visionary alderfolk of Burnham that something needed doing. Industrial parks were their solution. Modern units would attract new industry to Burnham, they proclaimed. The alderfolk set low rates and offered inward investment grants to get the scheme going. It was all launched on a wave of optimism. The few who knew which land the alderfolk were going to purchase for these industrial parks made a killing. The press marvelled at the scheme. But businesses were stubborn, unpersuaded they should move to a neglected, corrupt former mill town or decamp from the old mills that did as good a job more cheaply. The industrial parks scheme folded after only two new parks, Rose Vale and Merry Vale, were built.

Rose Vale was fifteen reclaimed acres of 1990s' yellow brick, its entrance directly opposite Burnham's main household refuse tip. The verges of the approach road were festooned with advertising boards that screamed the increasing desperation of the Park's remaining businesses: 'Kitchen Factory 50% off sale',

'DCT Container Makers Low Low Prices!!!', 'Mercury Transport & Storage. Any Quote Beaten. We Mean Any!', 'Klampdown Clothing Open to the Public', 'Burkes Hoses To Industry.'

Delroy drove up to the gates, scattering scavenger pigeons out of the way. The gates swung open automatically onto low-cut, gently contoured grass, and a badly metalled tarmac road lined with undernourished saplings. Rubber speed humps allowed five miles an hour. A lake of water covered grass and tarmac at the park road's pinch turn point. Delroy's Punto was bumped then bathed. The tarmac fanned out at the end of the road into a horseshoe arrangement of sheet glass fronted, corrugated metal sheds. Roller shutters down showed a unit occupancy rate edging 60 per cent.

In the horseshoe there were three stacks of newly welded steel containers, an abandoned heavy-duty fork-lift truck in grey and rust orange An old BMW, a 125 cc motorbike and some low reg Fords occupied the bays close to the unit entrances. The Reception unit had a canopy projecting out into the road. Delroy parked in the visitors' bay and made his way there.

A security guard in short-sleeved pilot's shirt, with neat, gold bar and black epaulettes, looked up from behind a sweeping semi-circular desk, and waited for him to approach. Delroy made his way slowly under the guard's scrutiny. Visitors seemed to be a real event these parts, at least visitors who reported to Reception. Delroy glanced at the name badge. Will Thomas.

-Hi,Will.

-Hi yourself.

A man after his heart, Delroy decided. The security guard folded his *Daily Mirror*.

-If you're selling 'owt, I'm not interested, said the guard.

Delroy smiled. -Nope. Could be I'm visiting someone. That's where I'm parked, the visitors' bay.

-And could be I'm the Dalai Lama.

Will had got him bang to rights, Delroy had to admit. He was a big guy with a friendly, mottled face and washed-out blue eyes. His greying hair was plastered to his head with some kind of hold-fast gel that had lost control of a few strands to the sides by his ears. He had a gold sovereign ring on a finger of one of his chubby hands. His hands were tucked into his folded arms, in classic fuck-off mode.

-You're quick, Delroy complimented him.

-People think security industry personnel are thick. I only missed MENSA by two points.

-I couldn't even work out how to fill in the form.

The guard liked that and it relaxed him. Delroy pressed on while the going was good. -My name's Delroy.

-How can I help you, Sir?

-I'm a friend of the family of the boy that died back there. You hear about it?

-Mebbe.

Will was closing down on him again.

-They asked me to see what I can do to maybe help them out, you know, the family, maybe, find what happened a bit more.

-Kind of you.

-They're paying me a little money for it. Were you here on that night?

-I might have been.

-If you were, I wondered if you saw anything on any of the, you know, the screens up there. There's a camera overlooking, I noticed.

A bank of six TV screens above Will Thomas was showing CCTV pictures.

The guard shook his head slowly and dipped his chin like Delroy had said something deeply ignorant.

-Doesn't work like that.

-How does it work then, mate?

-You see I'm faced this way, right, and they're behind me from here. Now, unless I'm gonna start cricking my neck, or doing my back in, I don't look unless the buzzer sounds and that button on the desk there lights up. If those two things happen, simultaneously mind, that means there's movement inside the fence or in some other unauthorised zone. Then I look. If it's night, it's usually my pepperoni pizza man coming to the side door.

-So you don't watch them, generally?

-They don't pay me to watch generally. They pay me five pounds 67 pence per hour before tax to react to alerts. Then reception here, signing them in, checking badges, which isn't too much late night, which is why I volunteer that shift. When it's quiet I flick through catalogues.

-To see what Ann Summer's bringing out for the spring? Delroy nodded to where a corner of the magazine just showed between the *Daily Mirror*.

Will Thomas opened out his *Daily Mirror*. The magazine title read called Max Hardware. -The mission is to build a Formula 1 PC for less than my monthly wage. On a par with Jesus and the loaves of bread, if I pull it off.

-Tell me about it.

Will smiled then.

-Yeah, I used to do this job.

-Yeh?

-Umm. Faxing in your timesheet and then them losing the things anyway and emergency taxing you. That still happen?

-All the time.

-Is those screens there wired to a computer?

-A hard-drive stores the images, if that's what you mean.

-And you never saw anything that night?

Will shrugged. -You look occasionally, but, grey is grey. There's the occasional fox, that's it.

-Why does it do that? Delroy nodded to the screens.

-What?

-The stop-start thing?

-Refresh. Every three seconds. Saves on storage.

-Could I take a look at the tapes for the night he was killed?

-Two police done that already.

-And?

-And they found fuck all, not even a fox.

-Just to be on the safe side?

-I'd have to knock out a camera feed to free up a screen.

-What about that one? You're not expecting some robber to swing in from the guttering in broad daylight are you?

Will Thomas tightened the fold of his arms. -See, I'd be risking my job, Sir.

The rise at the end of his voice and the open, hopeful eyes invited a negotiation.

-How about for twenty?

-It's a big risk.

-Thirty?

Reward outweighed risk at thirty quid plus twenty Superkings from the vending machine at the back.

Will Thomas knelt down to the control box under the Reception desk and got on it. The middle screen jumped, then blurred as the digital clock on the bottom left of the middle screen sped backwards. Finally they were at the date. Will worked the fast forward button while twisting round to watch the screen which was one big snow storm; taking it from 8pm he slowed enough so it was decipherable. Clouds zipped along but the building and surroundings were inert. Few people used the passage. A couple of dogs. A plastic bag blowing. Then it got darker. They got all the way to midnight, with nothing of remark, then two hours beyond and still nothing. Then daylight began creeping back onto the screen. Will paused it.

-Seen enough? he asked.

Disappointed, Delroy was ready to fold his tent. He glanced at the other screens. That was when he noticed it. What he could have kicked himself for not noticing before. It was staring him in the face.

-What date's on your *Mirror*? he asked.

-23rd, said Will.

-And what's the date on these screens?

-... 22nd. Yeh, some mistake there.

-How long's it been like that?

-They don't pay me to check the dates, Will replied.

Delroy couldn't help smiling. -What union are you in?

-They don't pay me to join a union neither, he deadpanned.

-Alright, Will. Rewind, rewind, go back one more night.

They sped through the daylight hours then watched again as darkness settled over the track. An old lady with shopping bags. A heavy-set guy with two Rotweillers. Past midnight, the shadows were heavy, the blur harder to make out. They both watched, fascinated, as in the murder time-frame a human shadow almost jumped into the frame of the screen, walking loosely like youth did, in the middle of the track's camber. It was hard to say whether it was an Asian or white or African-Caribbean youth. Like a grainy ghost, the figure moved along in time-delay jerks along. The hands swung, one hand wider than the other, the other hand clunky with something. Yes. The video camera, Delroy thought. It had to be Karim. As the figure reached the centre of the path, another figure entered the left side of the screen, in dark clothing, stockier, moving quickly behind the first figure, running maybe. It happened in not more than twelve seconds of screen time. A thrust with a hand by the second figure. Karim's half-turn, then fall, the other figure falling with Karim to the ground. A short struggle. A pause. Then the second figure moving off, leaving the first figure prone on the ground, twitching. The prone figure stayed like that, twitching.

-It takes training.

-What do you mean? asked Delroy, deep in thought.

-To reprogramme the date on the screen. Maybe I could do it right now but by rights they should send me on a training programme, like the bosses get.

-Shut up, Will, Delroy said.

-I was only...

-Wind it back a little.

-This is evidence, isn't it? We ought to call the cops.

He was excited: an ordinary man who never had anything happen in his job, suddenly finding himself in the middle of murder.

-Just give me a few minutes. I need the other tapes for the other cameras. Can you get them up?

Will Thomas declined. Delroy couldn't tell if it was fear or truculence. -You'll be a hero, he tried.

-A sacked hero.

-Not if you say you found this, on your own initiative. You'll be a hero.

Will softened. -They don't pay me to be a hero.

Twenty settled it.

The rear camera showed a white van pull up in the

street to the back of the unit almost half an hour before the murder. The definition was not high enough for a number plate.

Examining the CCTV of the track again, Delroy could make out the blur of the video camera falling out of Karim's hand. It did not look like the assailant took it with him when he fled.

He rewound again.

There were a couple of seconds after they had fallen to the ground, after the short struggle. At this point Karim was prone, not resisting, but the attacker hovered over Karim's upper body, he couldn't see why.

-Are we done now?
-Let it play on. I want to see what happened after.
-This can't...

Having no cash left, Delroy simply glowered at him. Most big people were cowards trapped in large bodies, he'd found.

-Alright, alright, Will relented.

A figure turned up in the dark hours of early morning, jeans, wearing a hooded top, white footwear, a lop-sided walk, the face hardly visible. The figure slowed, hesitated at Karim's body, kicked it tentatively in the side twice, then bent down and went through Karim's pockets. This done, it stood, looked around again, moved off to one side of the track then crouched, picked something up. Then it proceeded down the track quickly, breaking into a run that took it out of the camera's range.

Delroy took over the controls and played and replayed the section. Will protested. He took it frame by frame. The spill early on matched the pick-up by the interloper. He worked out the distances. It was the video camera the interloper had taken.

-I could sell ice-cream, the crowd we've had, Will moaned.

-One more thing.

-It's always one more thing.

Delroy had him bring to screen the tape for that murder night again. There was a van in shot on the street to the rear of the unit. It was a high-sided white van, standing, lights off around the time of the murder. It was driven away shortly after the stabbing by a stocky, blurred, male figure. There was no writing on the van's side and the number plate was not visible. You could not tell the make. It had ladders on its side.

Who worked or drove a white van at that time of night? It was too dark for installing double-glazing, or SKY dishes, or boarding up. Many white van drivers did use their work vans as private taxis too if they could get away with it, taking the wife shopping or clubbing, or bringing grandma round. If it was a local man, the van would show up again round about the same spot, and some other local might know the driver and where they lived.

Leaving Will to phone the police, and polish his hero lines for the press, Delroy went round and along the side paths. The side fire exit doors for all the units all had steel gates protecting them and some of these gates he passed were unlocked and the fire doors open. Delroy could hear workers' voices inside amidst a din of metal bashing.

The rear paths were only three yards from the high spiked, galvanised metal fencing, separated by a strip of marshy grass. He did a quick look by the fence but there was nothing. In his dreams he'd find the knife, but it was just that – dreams. Keen to get away before the Uniforms arrived, he walked back up, got into his

Punto and drove off the park and round to the street at the park rear where the white van had been. He got out of his car and walked along the track again. 'Some junkie' had reported the crime, Hilary Meadows had said. With no-one else on the footage in the time window, it was a fair assumption the same guy picked up the video camera. The guy had rung in with information. Addicts were not known for their sense of civic duty. The kind of path way it was, you didn't use it unless you knew that it was there, that it was short, where it led to, and you were familiar enough with it not to get panicked by its shadows and narrowness. So it was most likely a local. How would a local addict have disposed of a video camera? Addicts were not the world's greatest long-term planners. He knew this personally. For a junkie, it would be the fastest route to a fix. And in an area like this, West Burnham, that would be to sell the video camera to the nearest local charity shop.

He doubled back and walked off the path and into the surrounding streets, looking for junk shops. When all other trade ended, the junk shops staggered on. They were the scavenger birds of poor towns. When things looked up, they became antique shops, varnished everything and whacked up their prices. When times toughened, they got into everything from Auntie Agatha's Arthritis Miracle Cure to on-site Zimmer Frame Refurbishment. Their main competitors for goods received were the churches and the charity clothes collectors; and for goods sold the pub bag crowd, and the car boot sellers.

He worked through the streets in a loose, widening circle. A few corner shops doing cigarettes, bread, eggs and long-life provisions, a kebab shop doing no visible trade but taking phone orders, a newspaper shop with a couple of kids' bikes outside. He asked a cream-hatted lady out with her little wiry dog where he might find a junk shop around here, please. She recoiled at him and her dog yapped. A couple of youths came by in their finery. He didn't bother them. Even if they knew they would not be telling him that they knew. He smiled to himself imagining the reaction: 'You tellin me I look like I stepped out of a charity shop, Mister?' In the end a bow-legged, blue-suited gent walking his Labrador told him: left, second left, round the back, then right. He thought it was closed on Sunday, but gave him the directions anyway.

Delroy strolled on, taking in the sights. The teens and twenties Asian males were peacocks, dressed mostly Western style in pressed chinos, designer shirts and jackets. They glittered with jewellery and leant proprietarily on custom kit cars with lowered suspension and throaty exhausts. The old generation Asian men were more toned down. They wore baggy trousers and the traditional outsize, unshaped long cotton shirts in pale blue or black under their coats, the women wore wraps in black or other subdued colours, and their clothes were even more baggy and shapeless. He didn't have the key to this traditional Asian and Muslim dress code. Yet to the insider eye, he knew, there would be differences that gave clues to each wearer's personality and roots, clues in the embroidery, the pattern, the length, the way the shirt was worn.

His ears found the junk shop before his eyes. Deep-voiced shouts and exclamations. He came round the back and there they were: four old Asian guys, looking so similar they could be brothers, outside among scattered lounge furniture in freezing weather, each on their own odd junk-shop chair. The four of them had at least two hundred and fifty years between them. Delroy passed them then paused at the shop's side window, eavesdropping. What brought them to sit outside in double coats in weather like this? It was not even clear the shop was open. They paid him no attention. He heard them in their own language, without understanding. The mutterings and orations, the banging of the chipboard coffee table in emphasis reminded him of dominoes nights with the old-timers at the West Indian Centres. Their beards were different lengths and sizes. Did longer mean older or more religious? He guessed maybe the orange beard of the one on the rocker chair meant the possessor had just returned from his Haj – the pilgrimage to Mecca that every Muslim had a duty to make at least once in their lifetime. Junk outside, junk in the window and four bearded mullahs from Mirpur sitting on frozen junk, in animated discussion. What did they talk about. Back home? Religion? Family? Opening a new shop? The quality of the junk? He could only guess. He listened, tickled by the cadences, the rhythms.

He knew the language was most likely Punjabi. But Punjabi from what era? It was probably a fossilised version, the version they were speaking fifty years ago in Pakistan, the equivalent of '50s' English. They would be saying 'Blast!' and 'Dash it!' 'Crumbs!' and 'Are you kidding me?' Their children, the second generation, would speak some variant of this, updated by travel and Asian TV channels perhaps, and with a greater sprinkling of English. Then the third generation, brought up by the grandparents while their parents went to work, would be back using the grandparents' antiquities: 'Crumbs!' 'Balderdash!' exclaimed the three-year-old in Punjabi to her astounded mum. He smiled at the thought. It was all speculation. What was not speculation was the Panasonic MX 500 staring back at him in the centre of the junk shop window. Sometimes God smiled on you.

-Good day to you all, is the shop open? Delroy asked and waited. Somebody would speak English.

-Good day, Sir. What is it you like? said the orange-bearded man. He rubbed his knees supple and pushed himself out of his rocker. The other three, after a moment's interest, went back to their conversation.

-Erm, there's a few things in the window. This skates?

-Five pounds.

-This record player?

-Six pounds.

-And this camera. How much for this?

-How much you pay?

Good reply, Delroy acknowledged to himself. It put the pressure back on the buyer.

Most of England's shops had become a bar-coded scan zone, but there were still little places keeping alive the art of the haggle.

-Can I see it? he asked.

-Come.

The old man shouldered the rickety front door of the shop open.

Inside, ancient bric-a-brac was piled high. The man weaved his way through it all deftly towards the window and re-emerged with the video camera in one hand. From the way he held it out to him, wrong way up, Delroy assessed he did not know one end from the other. Delroy flipped the camera round and took a look. A tape was still loaded in it. He had to have it. He kept calm, for fear any show of interest would raise the price.

-Flat battery... Screen's gone, see? he said with a shrug.

-It's very new, the junk keeper countered.

-But does it work? Who knows? Delroy pursed his lips: -Twenty pounds. That's the most.

-Fifty.

-Forty?

He paid forty-five from his back-pocket roll and made a note to hit an ATM later, see if by any miracle he had any cash left.

Video camera purchased, Delroy drove straight to his church office. In the downstairs kitchen, washer-uppers were clattering away. He successfully sneaked past. Hallelujah.

His office was nothing you'd see on TV's 'Through The Key Hole', but it was comfortable. He'd inherited pink walls and a carpet like a moulting camel's back, buzzing fluorescent lighting encased in yellow, dead-fly lined plastic cases, a view of a hand carwash lot, and five different damp smells each to their own zone.

But he had a desk and chair, a filing cabinet, a TV, a phone line, a lamp, his three shelves of books on mainly Egyptian history, a stereo, a bed settee, and a Makonde sculpture on a window ledge, to prove he knew class when he saw it.

He cranked on the gas fire and waited for the flames to burn from yellow to red. Then he flipped on the desk lamp and sat down to take a closer look at his new purchase. He pressed the ON button, but nothing happened. It had a very small battery at its base. He flicked it off, dug out a multi-socket charger, checked the battery voltage, then hooked the charger to the battery plate. Green lights blinked. Bingo. He was away.

The video camera was no more complicated than a mini disk player and the buttons were actually bigger than on mini disk players. His big mitts worked the Panasonic's controls.

That evening he rejoined the congregation. Violet would have noticed the lights on anyway. Better to show willing. Evening worship was a different vibe to morning. More people came, mainly to eat and keep warm after the long, cold haul of day in their separate, draughty homes. Gusts of cooking escaped from the kitchen. If his nose was on the money, what was being prepared was the jollof rice concoction introduced by a visiting African and raised to an art form by the sisters. It tantalised his stomach. He sat at the back again. Nobody shoved up next to him. He knew he looked rough: unshaved, his shirt collar fraying and his shoes spattered with mud after tramping about at the back of Rose Vale Park. It was only when the congregation numbers reached the high sixties that his row began to fill. The singing began, ragged at first, then coming together and rising firmly in unison like oars on God's ship. The Minister had the helm and steered the choir for the heights, keeping them in time with firm chops of his ancient hands. His mouth opened as they reached a crescendo and he filled his lungs, sucked in the spiritual energy his choir generated, till he was no longer the frail old man with skin like bark, unsteady feet and cataract-filled eyes, but a colossus of faith, radiating power, ready with one sweep of his hands to clatter asbestos-ridden buildings to the ground, with another sweep to sort out the flooding sewage problems the town hall people never fixed. The choir ploughed on and the ship cleaved the waters.

In the pleasantly numb afterglow of the singing, with

the cooking smells ever more insistent, the Minister began his sermon. He started softly, fumbling for a strand, before settling on the Ninth Commandment and the parable of the Samaritan:

-And so this man, who found his enemy prone and laying there wounded at his mercy on the stony mountain path and yet he chose to help him! the Minister called.

-Yessir, the congregation responded.

-He could have walked on!

-Uhuh, the congregation agreed, urging him on with soft whispers.

-No one would have knowed, there was no-one around!

-Uhuh.

-But he didn't walked on by, he stooped and helped him up! He helped his enemy up!

-That's right.

-His enemy!

-Right!

-Though it would prolong his journey and increase his load yet those were not factors in his decision!

-No!

-Here was a needful person...

-Aah!

-Are we not all at some times in need? If I walk away from him today, might not the same thing happen to me tomorrow?

The Minister was gone into his trance. Delroy admired his fervour. In a world gone cynical it was healing to hear this. He himself had gone cynical. He was the man lying on the floor that needed a Samaritan to come by and lift him up. But nothing had happened in his world for him to get exalted about in a long time.

He had been good at soldiering. Discharged on health grounds, he got out to find his wife in bed with some painter and decorator. She claimed he was checking the ceiling tiles. He'd have laughed, if his tears had let him. Then came the booze, his stupidest move of all, and living out of his car and a bottle of spirits, and four dogs for company. The *Big Issue* doctor had saved him, he knew that. She had explained he had pancreatis: 'You'll die if you drink again,' she said. He'd come through alive and had touched hardly a drop since. But booze was like a lost lover, and even from the distance of memory, it overshadowed all his present pleasures. And neither Trudy, nor Violet, nor Susan had the exquisite warmth that came from a bottle. The bottle was supremely uncomplicated, it removed you from this world surer than a bullet in the head. The army had done that to him. Supplied that thinking, that vocabulary. Would he always feel out in the cold? At least he was getting familiar with the territory.

And the Karim case. His ten hours was up, but he was not doing the case on a meter no more. He usually did matrimonials. Spying on errant husbands. This was a completely different feel. Worthwhile. Instead of hiding in bushes outside Novotels with a telephoto lens.

The Minister lifted the choir again. His face agitated as he channelled spirits along every nook and cranny of his old body. He was the shaman, the apothecary, alchemising the gold of hope from the dross of life, wrestling the demons of despair to the ground and freeing the angels of faith till they thronged the old church hall. Delroy watched angels popping from the Minister's shoulders, watched them gather above him and spread out into the roof void of the church. He joined in the song trying the words of the chorus in his mouth for fit, loving this song that was a bonfire of demons, happy to sling his own demons on the pile:

Bind us together, Lord, Bind us together!
In robes of heavenly greatness!
Bind us together, Lord!

He wanted a way forward, a road through to justice. He wanted the Karim killer caught and locked up. The answer, the church Minister, the congregation was telling him, was faith. Faith in who?

Bind us together, Lord!

9

Hilary Meadows was ready for him at HQ reception, looking to all the world like he'd just swallowed a plate of sliced lemon. They shook hands briefly.

-I'm up to my neck in assessments, Meadows said to him through a forced smile.

-Morning to you, too, Delroy replied.

Meadows led him without squeaks this time, through the grey labyrinth of Burnham Divisional HQ. They made it to what could have been the same office room, only it was on ground level.

-This is the last time.

-Yeh, until the next last time.

-I can't do this. You said a tape. It's in that Aldi bag?

-I'm fresh out of Harrods bags.

Meadows glanced at his watch. -Give. Please. I'm asking nicely.

Delroy scooped the video camera out of the plastic bag. -I'll run it for you. It's technical. Come over this side.

Meadows dragged his chair round and sat alongside Delroy as the small LCD screen flickered to life.

-Notice the timer, Delroy said.

-It's all blurs. This is your breakthrough?

-Now watch... see? Wait. Now see here, here's the sky, watch the time. My theory is it's knocked almost out of his hand, and that triggers the play button, maybe he was filming sky before.

-You get all that from three blurs?

-Look! Just look. There! You see that?

-No. Meadows leaned closer.

-Wait. Delroy rewound four seconds of tape. -Right, watch again. Here it comes. There!

Meadows laughed. He put a hand on Delroy's back. -Find a dark room, Delroy, lie down, get some rest.

-You don't see it?

-There's nothing to see.

-Right, last time. Delroy rewound again and played it once more. -There. On the wrist.

-A bracelet? Dirt?

-You can just make it out. It's two bolts.

-You've lost me.

-Lightning or thunder. Two S's. The Nazi squiggles.

-Right. You've brought me away to look at squiggles?

The man was obtuse. Delroy saw horns growing out of the back of Meadows' head.

-We'll keep the tape and camera anyway, thanks.

-You don't have any ideas who it is?

-We'll look at it.

-What about this? Delroy tapped the videocamera itself. -Your 'mugger' left this expensive video camera, and they left jewellery.

-It was dark... Well?

-It was no mugging.

-Maybe he got disturbed. Spooked.

Delroy was vehement: -But the CCTV shows there was no-one anywhere near.

-Does it?

-You haven't seen it?

-We'll have someone on it soon. We'll edit it and show it the team. It's not easy. They have to bring down the overtime. They work to a budget. And what were you doing at Rose Vale?

-Your job, Delroy sighed. So much for faith.

Meadows took his chair back to the opposite side of the desk and sat.

-Anything else? he asked him with finality.

-There was a white van on the CCTV. Maybe you could get the plate number if you enhanced the tape? If you watched the tape?

-Yeah, right. That's what you want me to say?

-You could say yes.

-We have a plan, remember. We're applying it. Why don't you leave it to the professionals? All this busybodying, going through other people's bins, what's that? Get a life, Delroy, and get out of our way. Now, we're done. Meadows stood.

-About the Tourette's?

-What about it? Meadows bristled.

-I'm sorry if I said anything back then that, you know that... schoolboy stuff...

-It's all water, gone under, swept away. Don't trouble yourself. Now I've got a meeting.

-Still...

-You've got to stop calling on me here. We're taking this case seriously as you, Delroy. Believe me.

-I believe. Delroy rose and patted his stomach. -Any chance you have a canteen here?

Meadows whisked him out of HQ.

The van. It bugged him. Royd Street was not the kind of place you parked a van up when visiting Burnham. It was too isolated a street, a cul de sac that was too difficult to get to, too badly lit and without a fast enough escape route. The more he thought about the van, the more he wanted to know.

It was his old lifestyle, living out of a car and he resumed it as easily as slipping on an old T-shirt. He made up three flasks, one of sweet, hot coffee, one of hot tinned tomato soup and one of iced Red Bull and stuffed a rolled-up sleeping bag onto the back seat. He got to Royd Street for around 8pm and hunkered down in the driver's seat.

Dark soon rolled over him, and with darkness came a kind of trippy, Red Bull and coffee fired, waking sleep. He watched people and cars float by on the pavements and road. A few vans came, U-turned, and eventually went, but all the wrong size or colour. One or two people stared hard as they passed him near side, challenging his presence. He ignored them, refusing eye contact. Most left him alone with his personal stereo. Night soon blanketed him totally. He wound the Punto's front windows down two inches for air flow. Still, every half hour he wiped the windscreen clear of condensation.

As often happened when he waited like this, his deeper thoughts hit him, such as, why was he doing this job? Why was he dragging himself around, wallowing in other people's misery? Like Meadows said, what was he scared of? Where was the kick? Was it his own misery he was busy running from?

Two weeks back he'd seen Trudy waddling along at Hayrick Shopping Centre, bags in her arms, her stomach high. He had not been able to tell whether the tears in her eyes were perspiration or upset or both. He offered her a lift back to her flat and she invited him up. She told him she wanted to talk. They squashed together into the clanking steel lift. Inside her flat, the heating had been left on and a heatwave hit him. He sat there on her shell sofa, first thawing but soon sweating. As he sipped the juice she brought him, she talked:

-I'm not mad at you. Even though he's kicking me

fierce now, wanting to get out, I can understand your feelings. People say 'age ain't nothing but a number' but it is more than that. You get tired quicker, and you've lived enough to of worked out a routine that gets you through most things and you don't want the disruption. Well, it's the same with me, Del, I'm no dancehall queen no more, the dentist is talking to me about dentures, and I don't hardly recognise myself in the mirror – 'who's that old crone?'

-Don't say that, Trude.

-No, really, I'm an old broiler. And like you've got your routine, I've got my ways too. My toaster dial has to be set on five, my shower I want medium hot, toothbrush has to be in the middle of the rack facin' out, you know? I know where you're coming from. A baby comes along on the horizon, you're afraid they're going to wreck your routine, and you don't have the knees no more to be crawling on the carpet playing piggy back. That's what you're thinking right, you know? And the baby's going to need you intently and you don't like that, you don't like anyone needing you, right?

-Don't cry, I'm not worth it.

-And everyone knows black men run, right, from commitment. That's what my friends say.

He put an arm around her shoulders. -Hey, I'm here.

-I remember when... I... my first baby... It's just... I'm keeping this one. I'm keeping this one, not giving it away or having it suctioned. Back then, I couldn't... I was not fit to be a mother, I look back and I can see it now, I'm not ashamed of it, it's there in my past. I was too young... I wasn't ready.

-You don't need tell me all this, Delroy soothed.

-One day, maybe she'll seek me out, and, maybe she'll understand, maybe she won't. She could be cold to me, or she could put an arm around me and say, 'I still love you, Mum.' Whichever way, I prepare myself for that, every day.

She nudged Delroy's arm from her shoulders.

-When you feel you're ready, she said, -if you ever feel you're ready, this child I'm carrying is yours and we'll both still be here... You don't need a blood test to say it's yours, do you?

-No, Delroy said softly.

She stared at him intently for a moment, making him squirm. Then she looked away towards the front window with the drawn vertical blinds. -Sometimes, I lie awake or I'm dreaming, the stage you get when you're not sure which.

-Dozing?

-Yeh, and she appears before me, my daughter, she comes into my bedroom. She bends down and touches my face. Sometimes she brushes it gently, other times she pinches it, hard, on the cheek. Always then, I'm cold awake, light on, pacing. Then the dream fades... When she's here, her face always looks the same. Not the spit of me, not the spit of her dad, she's her own self... She's eighteen, intelligent, charming, but when she's alone with me all of that drops off and she's beautiful but like a diamond is beautiful: the core of her is hard, when she looks at me.

He didn't know what to say. -You'll be OK, you'll get on...

She sobbed quietly. -Don't worry, it's just dirt under my contacts, I guess you've got to go now, I guess you have things to do?

How could he say he had things to do when she was in this state? But he didn't have words. He was unused to the situation.

She sobbed quietly -Say something, Del, don't sit there like a lump of stone, don't do that to me...

-Trude I know you've had it hard, but... don't beat yourself up over things, you know?

-... The worst thing would be she shows up and she looks me in the eye and goes, 'You gave away another baby, didn't you? Or did you have it sucked out of you? Is that what you meant to do with me, but you left me in your womb too late? Is that it?' What would I say to her then? I keep this baby and she can come round and play with her. 'You've got a little sister,' I can say. 'Look – your sister – isn't that great?'

-I understand, Trude, I understand.

-...You can go now.

-I didn't mean...

-It's OK. I've got my troubles, you've got yours. Please, go, I'll call you, Del.

He hugged her, then left her unpacking her shopping.

The street remained vacant of high-sided white vans. He had finished the Red Bull, but the coffee was still good.

Why was it he ran from commitment like a grizzly for the hills? Why had he not said the words she wanted to hear? What she had said that evening had stirred something in him. It was as if she had supplied him with a language for his feelings. Yes, he was getting old. Yes, he felt afraid of breaking his routines. Was that why he ran? He shifted uncomfortably in the Punto. The car he'd lived out of at the lowest point in his life had been a red Ford Sierra. This was a tiny Punto. Even with lower seat slid furthest back and the upper section wound down, his back ached.

Shafiq Amin rang, checking on progress. It was early

days, he told him. He rang his office machine and picked up a message about a missing girl from a potential new client. He'd have to hang fire on that. Meadows rang him to say yes, the CCTV had caught a white van but no, the number plate was never visible and enhancement would serve no purpose, the recording was too poor quality.

The coffee finished.

Early morning flared up and Delroy watched a tiny, red-chested bird land on a bush growing wild over a front yard wall. An Accuread meter reader got short shrift from three of the houses he called at, then was waved in by a fourth. A debt collector sailed up the street with an official-looking clipboard, in short sleeves, grey shirt, delivering no-nonsense raps on doors. He called on three houses, collected, then drove off in a Ford Fiesta. Delroy yawned, then swigged grainy dregs of coffee from the flask. He felt sweat drying at the back of his neck and felt the crawl of his growing beard. He scratched his chin then rubbed the corners of his eyes. Surveillance was stamina through monotony. There had been no white van, all through the night.

He got out, stretched his legs and knocked on some doors asking after the van. Sometimes he had to ask the kids in the house to translate his questions for the elderly relatives looking after them, then translate the answers. The upshot of his door-stepping was nobody they knew owned a white van, nobody drove a white van and nobody had seen a white van parked there in the evening; there was a vegetable rounds man who had a big red van but that was it. He walked some more, happy at least to stretch his legs. He bought a pack of Eccles cakes from a corner shop and went back to his

Punto.

Next evening he resumed his vigil. Night thickened quickly. He stared on through the black. 2am and there was still nothing. He wondered about Violet. The thought meandered, the way his thoughts often did when they were about Violet, from her dinners to her scriptures. He was not a man for organised religion. He had been brought up a Christian, but if he had been born in Egypt, would he not have been a Muslim? Or in Delhi become a Hindu? It was all an accident of birth. He accepted what the religions shared, their belief in a spiritual dimension to life, their commitment to peace and harmony as ideals. But adopting one creed and living out its particular rituals and commandments? He was the waverer everyone wanted to convert. He'd get talking at a kebab shop and be offered salvation in Allah's arms. He'd be looking for a pair of shoes in a charity shop and be handed a leaflet for a service at a Sally Army Hall. Why were the Sally Army so into uniforms? If you liked uniforms that was your religion. If you wanted suits, you headed for the Mormons. You wanted big hats, you went to the Seventh Day-ers. His thoughts meandered in this way through the small hours.

The van never reappeared. Either they were all lying, or they'd all missed it and he'd chosen the wrong evenings to maintain observations, or the van was from out of town. Two nights was enough.

He went back to his office, washed himself downstairs in the church kitchen, shaved and swapped clothes. Then he sat down to an oats and cold milk breakfast. There was no point talking to the police about the van, he knew, Meadows had made that clear. He had to change tactics.

-Hello Delroy, good to see you.

-Whap'n Stevie.

-Been working a graveyard shift?

-Sometin' like that. You're no hairspray ad yourself.

-True, she grinned. -Come through, come through.

Stevie was an old school socialist. She lived in a huge Victorian house on the Burnham-Manchester border. Her long, yellow hair was tangled at the back like she'd been plumbing a sink. She had on a double-check shirt, green designer combats and black monkey boots.

She led him along a corridor with a grandfather clock and eggshell walls and dado rails, into the kitchen. The kitchen was big enough to row a boat around in. Textbooks and photocopy papers strewn on the table where he'd been hoping to find biscuits, fruit, maybe a rack of toast. He noted the scrubbed-up natural wood floorboards and clever hidden lighting and flush fitted steel units.

-I've got Chinese, apple blossom... Spearmint?

-How about FineBrew?

-Ah, FineBrew. Problem. They're part of the Border-Gide organisation. They don't pay minimum wage in India and...

-OK, give me coffee. Make sure it's Cafe Direct, mind?

-Good on you.

-I didn't know college lecturers got paid so good, he said, looking about mischievously. All socialists felt guilty about their wealth.

-I wrote a few things in my spare time, Stevie

squirmed, -for the academic market and they kind of mainstreamed and before I knew it there were three extra noughts sitting in my bank account. What can you do?

-Next time you've got spare time, write me a book, Delroy teased.

-I will, she said, taking him seriously. She gave him his coffee. -What brings you here?

-I need to pick your brains.

Stevie was a member of the Burnham Anti-Racist Network. BARN kept up video, photography and eye-witness surveillance on local fascist groups. She was a demon with a loud hailer, and claimed she invented the Mexican chant, where a suitable slogan such as 'Down With Fascism' was started at the front of a march and was shouted serially in a Mexican Wave till it rippled all the way to the back of the march then made its way forward again.

Delroy told her about the Karim case.

-Can you help?

She scowled. -You know my position on this, Delroy. The only way forward is direct mass action. It is bourgeois individualism to spotlight an individual case, you're surrendering to the cult of personality which is late capitalism's dialectical response to the twenty-first century's technology-led democratisation of modes of communication.

-Whoaa, Stevie. Run it past me again, in English. Are you willing to help or not?

-With reluctance, and deep misgivings.

-That's a yes?

-Yes.

-Bet your book people pay you by the word.

She started to say something, thought the better of

it, said instead: -What pointers have you got so far to his identity?

He told her about the knife, the CCTV, and the tattoo, and the van. -From what I saw, I'd say no older than thirty, Delroy concluded.

-OK. Let's go to the Godhead, she said.

She unearthed a laptop computer at the head of the kitchen table, folded its lid up and powered it on.

-White van, white van, white van, she mumbled as she clicked away. She tapped the LCD screen. -There's three likely's. Mid-twenties you said?

-My guess.

-That leaves two. And the tattoo. Here you go.

The laptop processor fan whirred away and the screen refreshed strip by strip from bottom up, until Delroy was staring at a face. The caption below it read Gregory Gresty.

 -Never heard of this one before, she said, -but here's the full file. Lives on the Cherry Tree estate, works at Aardvark Alarms on Old Burnham Road. He's not been on the scene more than eighteen months, member of the Wrecking Crew. We picked him up at a football match. Photos are recent. That's all we've got on him. Any use?

-It's smoking. Brilliant.

She looked pleased. -Shall I print it off for you?

-Thanks.

-We have much more on the established characters, she said apologetically, handing him the print-out.

-Stevie, it's great, really. I'd kiss you, but you'd say it was decadent individualism.

-Thank the BARN team, not me.

He drank the coffee then made his excuses. They shook hands at the front door.

-There's an anti-deportation march through the town centre next month. Bring your family, it'll be a good, non-violent day out.

What family? Delroy thought, but he took the leaflet. You couldn't meet Stevie without taking leaflets. They were the sacraments of the radical left faith.

-Delroy, don't get me wrong. I hope you nail the bastard, she said, as he turned to go.

-I know that.

Back at his office, he spread the print-outs out on his desk. Stevie's laptop inkjet printer had eliminated any grey from the photograph reproduction so it was black or white. Gregory Gresty. He looked harmless enough. Black hair cropped short, chunky forehead and chin, flat nose, and prominent lips for a white guy. Nothing you would look twice at. One of the lads at a football match. But then, what did he expect: horns and a tail? In another photograph they had caught the tattoo on the forearm. Was this guy involved in the murder? It was a big leap.

He pushed the print-outs around on his desk, reading off the address, the guess at his height and weight, the colour of eyes and read some newspaper clippings on run-ins with the law involving other family members from ten years back.

He thought about Stevie and the anti-fascist old guard. They put years in knocking up placards, standing on street corners in sleet and rain with petitions, pounding pavements with leaflets and megaphones, knocking doors on estates, organising marches, standing on terraces taking photos. They kept tabs on the fascists so the younger generation had the freedom to not concern themselves with any of it. Mocked as ideologues and obsessives, they kept guard. Every community needed them. It was a pity most of them lived in trendy areas instead of at the heart of the tough mill towns where they were needed most.

Delroy considered his options. He could call at Gregory Gresty's home address, but that would not achieve much, or he could... His thoughts were interrupted by noise. His office walls began shaking to the sound of the choir below. They were stopping and starting like someone kept lifting the needle on a record. Unable to concentrate, he went downstairs.

They looked at him in mid song. He must have had a startled expression on his face.

-Practice night! one of them called when they had finished the bar.

-Carry on, don't mind me, he said.

He sat unobtrusively at the corner of the last row. For some reason his presence made them sing a full song. Maybe they mistook him for a rival choir leader or a visiting minister. Whatever the reason, they were in full voice now and it got the hairs standing on the nape of his neck.

Onward Christian Soldiers,
Marching as to war...

At first he heard only the British Empire words, the sabre rattling of the Christian priests crusading against the Moors. But the lyrics soon faded and it was the spirit of the singers that came through. A band of old-timers belting out the tune with a ragged fervour, punching through notes, rattling along the verse in their halting tempo, heads tilted back, faces shining with Holy sweat, ancient eyelids forged together. Where were they going in the song? They had spent a lifetime chasing the immigrant's dream of El Dorado in the UK. Now here, within these sagging walls, they were still marching towards that dream. Their singing roughed up Delroy's heart, made strange images collide in his imagination. Two container ships passing in a watery Atlantic night. A cage of pet-shop Mynah birds suddenly released and circling. Two friends holding hands in old Kingston heat. Coils of iron chains. A ghost slave trader ship. A procession of Egyptian pharaohs ascending into a purple sky. And he saw the church suddenly in gold: every trailing wire, every chipped wood chair and every cracked patch plaster job all gilded gold. The music rolled over him, his soul submerged in a river that had been flowing since the Nile first flooded the Egyptian plains.

In this mood of hope, he prayed: to God the one, the many, he prayed for an angel, a messenger, to come and help him with the Karim Amin case.

The choir faltered, then faded, and the exalted singing was replaced by the rasp of the choir leader's corrections:

-Mid-section, you're missing your cues. Again please.

The choir restarted again and was almost immediately pulled up again.

-Lagging, lagging, lagging! the exasperated choir leader berated them.

Delroy got up from the back bench and quietly removed himself upstairs. There, he sat at his desk again and batted ideas to and fro in his head. He did believe there was a right move out there, if only he could figure it out. He had Gregory Gresty's home address. He could try bumping into him at his local pub or wherever, but the chances of making more than a moment's contact were remote. No Wrecking Crew member was going to voluntarily pally up with a black man in public. That left his work place...

10

The next morning Delroy headed for Aardvark Alarms. He had put in some phone calls. The Aardvark Group had a reputation for scaremongering leaflets, and competent but overpriced alarms work. A sister company to Aardvark Alarms, Aardvark Services, listed its services as debt negotiation, refinancing, witness protection and patrol services. Aardvark Alarms was run by a cousin of the Aardvark Group head man. It traded from heavily shuttered, old premises located on an island of derelict land beside Burnham Old Road, some two hundred yards down from the first of Burnham Old Road's three speed cameras. The parade of shops that had been attached to the premises to the left side facing, had been pulled down and the ground compacted into a car park.

Delroy drove past at 9.16am. The car park was cluttered with white vans. A panoply of cheap, ridged plastic signs were hung in the shop windows and affixed to the side elevations:

Alarm Fitting. 6 Zones £195.

New Blinds £119 For Three.

Delroy turned into the car park, squeezed his Punto between two white Transits and headed for the front door. Pushing down the handle set off a chime. Aardvark's front office was cramped and humid. Straight on to him was a desk. There was another desk to the side with a woman with big auburn hair behind it who smiled at him, but behind the first desk sat a man with slow eyes. He was mid forties, had short, mousy hair, a copper face, and a Burt Reynolds moustache. He raised his eyes eventually and coolly sized Delroy up. The floor was marble effect lino.

-How may I help you?

-It's about the job, Sir, in the Job Centre they said they'd ring me through, only I wanted ter see yous meself so you can see how keen I am. I've done all kinds of alarms fitting and I'm not afraid of heights, an' I know my way round wiring and...

-Hold it there, squire. There is no vacancy.

-But the Job man said...

-Then the Job man got is wrong.

-You could take me on, on trial like, without pay like, for a couple a weeks, let me prove myself.

The free labour offer seemed to turn a key in the man's mind.

-What's your name again, sonny?

-Sylvester. Sylvester Small. My friends call me Silver.

-Hi ho Silver?

-Just Silver.

-Why should I take you on, Sylvester? There's hundreds out there, just as keen.

-Like I said, I'll work the first weeks free, gentleman's agreement like, you know, off the books. You don't want me after the month, no probs.

-One gentleman to another? Mr Burt Reynolds asked, amused.

-S'right.

-Take a seat, Sylvester.

Delroy sat in the plastic seat in front of Mr Burt Reynolds' desk.

-My name's Mr Hargreaves. Here at Aardvark, we don't sell alarms, we sell peace of mind.

-'Course. Everyone's good for a piece of that.

-Every customer must be not just happy, but delighted.

-Like clean the windows while we're up there?

-Exactly. And there are a number of extras we like to draw to our customers' attention. We call it the upgrade path...

Delroy allowed himself to be informed of the Aardvark Bronze, Silver and Gold upgrade paths. He then recited them back to Hargreaves. There was an amount of banging coming from below the lino and floorboards during all this.

-Don't mind the noise below, it's just the lads, getting their stock sorted for the vans. Do you have any qualifications in electrics?

-NVQ combined plumbing and wiring, Delroy lied.

-There won't be any plumbing. Unless you drill through a water pipe, Sylvester, Hargreaves said. He waggled his Reynolds moustache at his own joke, a trick Delroy thought worthy of applause in itself, though he left it at a broad smile.

-How would you feel about working on Asian houses?

-I worked on Victorian and Tudorian, but not Asian. They made out of bamboo?

-I'll do the jokes.

-Sorry, Mr Hargreaves.

-Well?

-Asians don't trouble me and I don't trouble them, see?

-Good. Well, we'll see how you get along, Sylvester.

-Thanks for the opportunity, Mr Hargreaves.

-On the basis you suggested, of course.

-Of course.

-Welcome to Aardvark Alarms. Hargreaves tilted

himself up two inches out of his black upholstered swivel chair and extended a soft, wet hand which Delroy shook vigorously.

-We'll see who we can pair you up with. Er, Janice? he called across to his colleague, -you haven't finished them rotas yet have you? Can you squeeze Mr Sylvester here in? He's on trial and I'll be, er, handling the paperwork myself. Hargreaves winked conspiratorially at Delroy.

Janice, rubbed a space clear on the rota white board behind her and pretended to grumble: -You really ought to give me a little more notice, Larry.

-I know, I'm sorry, Larry replied, with another wink to Delroy.

-Who do you want to put him with, darling? Janice said.

-With a G, Delroy cut in.

-Pardon, Sylvester? Janice said.

-Put me with anybody with G in their name. G's my lucky letter. And three's my lucky number.

-How interesting, said Janice. She glimpsed over to Larry Hargreaves with a roll of her eyes that said, 'This one needs a brain scan.' -It's your lucky day, Mr Sylvester, she said to him, -we have a G – Gregory. But you'd be a two, not a three.

-Two's good, Delroy said.

-You sure you don't want him on leafleting, Larry? Janice asked pointedly.

-Let's see how he gets on for now, Hargreaves replied.

She wrote 'Sil' on the board next to where she had written 'Greg'.

-I'll pop down and let Greg know, said Hargreaves. -Fill Sylvester in on timekeeping, will you? He rose from his chair. There was a white door built into the partition wall. Hargreaves pushed the handle down and the door swung back. The clatter of objects being thrown against hard surfaces rose from beyond the door.

-Greg? Hargreaves called, -you down there? Then he ducked down, swinging the door closed behind him. Janice continued with her black dry-wipe marker, her back to Delroy, while giving him the Aardvark essentials on timekeeping: -We gets our bonus every month, right, depending on hitting targets. Too long on one job means less bonus.

-Right, Delroy said.

From below there was a clatter of feet on stairs and a slosh of male voices. Looking out through the office side window, Delroy saw half a dozen men in green Aardvark pullovers emerge, toting tool kits, and cross the car park for the vans.

Delroy stepped quietly over to the cellar door and eased it ajar and listened:

-You've teamed me up with a nig, that's what.

-Aardvark is an equal opportunities employer, Hargreaves protested.

-Yeah, like I'm Robbie fuckin' Williams. What's the split? Fifty, fifty?

Someone was tutting. Delroy looked round. Janice.

-I thought maybe to go down and help, Delroy said, -but it don't sound like good timing. He walked back to his seat. -That our one? He pointed out of the side window to the only van left in the car park.

Janice nodded. -You driven a Transit before?

-Yeh. Like tanks, ain't they? he grinned.

Hargreaves and Greg came up from the cellar together

and Hargreaves introduced them to each other. There was a cursory nod from Greg that Delroy mirrored. Hargreaves handed Greg the Transit keys. Greg led and Delroy followed. They crunched across the car park to the van. They drove in silence to the first job. Delroy watched the world go by from the side window. He had no problem with silence right now. The lad would thaw, given time. Fifteen minutes later, they pulled over at an address on the Harbour Estate. Delroy whacked his interior side door handle open and jumped out, Greg did the same.

-Don't fuck about, just watch and learn, I know this job, Gregory said at the rear doors as he unloaded the tool kit.

-Fine by me, Gregory, Delroy replied.

-It's Greg. Not Gregory.

-Right. Greg.

Delroy had picked up some sparks skills in the army and he knew his ring circuit from his spur, but he let Greg take the lead on the jobs they did that morning. Greg talked gruffly or not at all, but he worked hard and he did neat jobs. The customers on Greenslade liked his efficiency. By touching one o'clock, they had done three jobs at separate addresses and were due a lunch break. As they piled their tools once more into the back of the Transit, Delroy said:

-My stomach's rumbling. What do you say to a doner kebab?

-I'll find us a chippy.

-You treating me then?

-No way, Greg said.

Greg pulled the van up across the road from a chip shop.

-I'll come with, Delroy said, -I like to go through the

menu, you know, see what they've got.

-You're having pie and chips and you're waiting in the van. Greg jumped down.

-Make that a steak pudding! Delroy called.

The driver's door slammed. Delroy watched Greg walk off. Stubborn bastard, he thought. Given time, he'd crack him. But how much time did he have? Five minutes later, Greg was back and jumped into the driver's seat. He tossed Delroy a chips bag, put his own bag on the dash among the bookie pens and fuses, knocked the Transit into first gear and sped off again.

-Lovely these, Greg, top one, pal.

-Let's just get this straight, we're not pals, we're not mates, and you owe me three pound twenty.

-Only trying to be friendly, like... What's the next job?

-Mr Faisal Malik, Greg said, then the address.

They were in an Asian area. It was not far from Freeham, where Karim's family lived.

They knocked.

Mr Malik was a thin, stooped, sandy-faced man in his sixties, whose shabby suit washed around him like he had been recently ill. His teeth when he smiled his greeting were reddy brown. His ramshackle appearance was in total contrast to the beautifully renovated hallway behind him.

-Aardvark Alarms, Greg began, -here to fit the alarm.

Mr Malik switched a chewing pouch into a cheek. -Good, thanks indeed. Come in.

Greg stayed on the doorstep. -How do you mean to pay?

-I have cash, Mr Malik replied, feeling his wallet in his jacket's inside pocket

-I have to take the money before we start work, Greg said bluntly.

-I pay soon as you finish.

-We're not allowed to start work till we have the money, Greg said.

The West Burnham stand-off, Delroy thought. Going on right now on the doorsteps of a thousand households.

Mr Malik held his ground. -You do the job, I pay, he smiled redly.

-Great. But we need the money up front, Greg continued.

The 'no' wrinkles deepened on Mr Malik's head.

Greg sighed. -Money. You understand English? I don't have all day.

Delroy stepped forward. -Mr Malik you have a lovely hallway, can we step through? Genuine alabaster coving?

-My son cast it from the original.

-You do want the job done? Delroy asked.

-Yes.

-Today?

-Yes.

-Then we need to move things on, don't you think, Mr Malik? Delroy said.

Mr Malik shrugged his agreement.

-Here's how we can do it. Why don't I write you an IOU for the amount, then you hand over the cash. We do the job and you check it. If you're happy with it, and only if you're happy with it, you hand me back my IOU. What d'you say?

Mr Malik gestured uncertainty with a hand.

Delroy smiled. -This way you're covered. You can sue on the IOU if you think we done a bad job.

Mr Malik relented. -Yes, OK. For you, OK.

Delroy wrote the IOU out on the back of an unopened Fast Loans envelope Mr Malik handed him off his hallway table. All three of them in the hallway knew the IOU he was writing was worthless. But it was a face saver for Mr Malik. Delroy signed it with a flourish. -Only one more thing, he said, handing over the IOU.

-What is that? Mr Malik asked.

Greg looked at him wondering too.

-Tea! Delroy exclaimed. -The British worker does not work without tea.

Faisal Malik laughed. -Of course, of course! He went off down the hallway towards his kitchen.

-Asians. They fuck about too much, Greg murmured. -By the way the rules are, never start a job for Asians without getting the cash from them first.

-Can't stand 'em myself, Delroy floated. -Fuck the Asians, right? he said softly, offering Greg his fist to knock.

-Right man! Greg replied, knocking fists.

The irony of this shit, Delroy thought. He always found it funny how some white people expected black people to side with them against Asians. Of course none of them had read Angela Davies's book, 'If they come for me in the morning, they'll be coming for you in the evening.' Then again, none of today's black kids had read that book either, in fact most of them had never heard of Angela Davies. Sign of the times.

Mr Malik came back with tea and a small bundle of notes. He handed over the notes to Greg. Greg made a show of checking each one with a counterfeit detector pen.

-No offence, like. Any fakes and it's subbed from our

wages.

-I have a machine downstairs. I print them there, Mr Malik said.

-Yeah? Greg eyed Mr Malik.

-You do a spot at the Comedy Club, right? Delroy said to Mr Malik.

-Every Friday, he smiled.

Greg took the lead again on the job, a wire-free system with four movement detectors, and front and rear couple of magnetic door contacts. Delroy passed tools, held ladders and, on Greg's call, tested the movement detector range. They had it done and dusted before the second tray of tea arrived. As Delroy supped his sugary brew, Greg bundled the tools into the back of the Transit. They set off for the next job.

By the time the working day was over, they had managed to squeeze in four more jobs. It meant a fat bonus for Greg, and he was in good spirits.

He took Delroy to West Burnham's Dog and Partridge. It was located on a street bright with the flash of Asian youth's cars. A new Asian community centre stood opposite, and Asian people hung outside the Centre. Any Asian entering the Dog would be observed and scandalised, Delroy guessed. Greg sauntered up the pub steps. Delroy's earlier guess was proved right: there was not one Asian in the pub, which was virtually empty.

A yellow-haired, middle-aged white man in a sixties' suit that had the wear to prove it sat at the bar nursing a pint and that was it, apart from the landlady. Delroy nodded to the bloke, then got Greg's lager and himself a blackcurrant and took them over to their table. He passed Greg his pint and placed his own on the table.

-What's that? Greg asked, indicating his drink.

-Rum and black, he lied.
-Girl's drink that, he declared.
-No better drink than rum, Delroy said, refusing to be riled.
-We ain't so bad a team, Delroy said.
-For an old man, you keep up, Greg allowed.
-Less of the old. You like this job then? Delroy asked.
-It's alright.
-Why don't you join the other lot? You've got the physique.
-Which lot's that?
-Aard Services. I heard it pays better.
Greg smiled. -The Ard Gang?
-How did that come about?
Greg dutifully explained. -The alarms lark is a good earner, but you see the boss's problem, what happens if they don't pay? Do you let them have the kit for free? Specially Asians. It's in the culture like, with Asians. 'Sorry, no money. You take half?' The Ard Gang go in, slash a few tyres, knock over some plant pots, maybe break a window, customer sees sense. Greg rolled his shoulder muscles. -I could join. It's not a craft though, is it?
-It is actually. They're running courses on it at Burnham College.
-Yeh?
-Diplomas in Bouncing, Biffing and Bodyguarding.
Gregory chuckled and stood. -You're a funny guy. I've got to get on.
Delroy knocked back his drink. -Your round next time.
-I'll drop you off at the office, said Greg.
-Nah, put me down near your place by Cherry Tree, there's a bus straight from there. You keep the van

overnight anyroad, right?

-How d'you know where my place is?

Shit. -Mr Hargreaves told me, Delroy lied. -Must have said in passing, like. Heydale, ain't it?

-What else did Hargreaves tell you about me? said Greg, curious.

-If I was gonna learn alarms, you wrote the manual.

This seemed to amuse Gregory.

The first week Delroy made steady progress. He laughed at Greg's jokes, praised his wiring skills (he *was* good) and went from the occasional friendly punch on the chest to throwing the occasional arm around his shoulder. He learnt his full name from his signature on the completion forms: Gregory Gresty, he learnt about Greg's would-be girlfriend, Angela, abut his gym fitness routines, and about his love of all things to do with Burnham AFC. Unexpectedly for Delroy, by the middle of the second week, Greg was coming across to him as a lonely but basically OK young man: the kind of young guy that the army, with its ready-made squad of friends in barracks, was ideal for. All this progress was on the work front, though. Greg kept his social life rigidly separated off from Delroy. They never stopped at any of the East Burnham pubs that were anywhere close to the football stadium, and at the end of a working day he never dropped Delroy off anywhere near his home, either because he did not want to have to invite Delroy in, or because he did not want to be seen there with this black man, or both.

Late afternoon on Thursday of the second week, they landed in East Burnham's Shoulder of Mutton. It had been a good day. They had worked out a modus operandi for the alarming that was making them one of the fastest teams at Aardvark. Greg's bonus was taking on mammoth proportions in his imagination. The Shoulder was near empty.

-Is the beer off or summat? Greg quizzed the bouffant-haired gargoyle of a landlady.

-More of your lip, and you'll be off, she fired back.

-Deep down you love me though, darling, eh? Greg winked at her.

He brought the drinks over to Delroy. Greg spent the first five minutes doing some time-sheet arithmetic in the margins of a discarded tabloid. -We keep this up and we'll be top team for the month. Numero Uno. I'll get the two hundred, he announced.

-How much of that will be mine? Delroy asked. He felt he ought to say something, and besides, he was actually short of money.

-I'll see you right, don't worry.

-That sounds like fifty-fifty.

-Nudging.

-Nudging?

-I'll see you right, I'm no tight fist, you've been alright.

-If that was a compliment I can't wait to be insulted.

-Here. In a magnanimous gesture, Greg rolled back his sleeve and showed Delroy his *SS* tattoo.

Delroy looked impressed. He could see Greg was nervous about showing it to him, under the bravado. -That done recent?

-Couple of months, like.

-A good line.

-Don't get me wrong. I'm no Nazi, like, it's just Pakis I hate.

-Why didn't you get 'I hate Pakis' done, 'stead then?

Greg thought about it a moment. -This was cheaper!

he said, finally, but he was uncomfortable. -'Fuck the Pakis'. That'll be the next one, he vowed.

-Right. Let's finish this last job, yeah? Delroy said, slapping him on the back.

The file on Gregory Gresty was looking good. Greg worked with his right hand, as had the Karim killer. He had the use of a white van after work. And he had the tattoo. But he could hear Meadows complaining: it was all circumstantial.

That evening, he pulled out the sofa bed in his office in the church but sleep eluded him. He opened the windows hoping to be lulled by the random sounds of the road. A stiff night breeze rolled in, carrying with it the smell of unburnt petrol, frying oil and damp mortar. He heard a cursing drunk collide into the roller shutters of the unisex hairdressers opposite, HGVs working through their gears to negotiate the road's incline. There was a lull. Then a boyfriend and girlfriend row outside the chip shop further up the road. Stragglers leaving some late-night mosque function. The night air rolled over him, heavy with sighs, and with it, finally, came sleep.

The carnival masquerade passed. Thousands of Nubian women wearing the blazing sunshine, wicked hairstyles and little else. A band of dancing pharaohs prancing on the road, bringing to belly-shaking life the ancient African Queens; the white-masked, ghost stilt dancers careering toward him, scaring the jerk chicken almost back up his throat; the short and bearded reggae artist on the lorry's float, his three tall, high-voiced Wailers swaying like thin palms as they sang covers of Bob Marley hits to a fuelled-up, blissed up, dark crowd. And the only face he remembered among them was Trudy and the big coconut and salt kiss they had shared.

Rocking Trudy in his arms as the red sky fell and the bass thumped its vibrations into the ground so the earth they were standing on shook. Where was he in his dreams? Was this Rio? Was this Trinidad? Was this Notting Hill?

Next day a fierce cross-wind was blowing and Delroy had to lean his full weight against the base of the ladder while Greg did the fixing. It did not stop Greg from supping tea from a mug, and admiring the little herb garden the owner had got going in pots.

Suddenly there was a curse from the top of the ladder: -Fuck! Fuckfuckfuck!

Then a clank: heavy steel hitting aluminium.

Delroy ducked. A cordless drill, its drill bit spinning maniacally, skewed past his head and smashed into an herb pot, splitting it.

-Fuck!... Fuck!

Delroy leaned hard into the ladder as it slid to the left. He managed, just, to arrest the ladder's slide before it skidded across into the window glass and calamity.

-Greg, you OK? he called up.

Gregory came down the ladder fast. He jumped the last five rungs and stood clutching his left hand with his right, cursing. His left hand oozed blood.

-Bastard drill slipped on the mounting plate! he said, showing Delroy his damaged hand.

It was a mess. The drill had gouged the inside of Greg's upper left thumb and a two-inch wide, inch-deep flap of flesh hung loose. Under that, Delroy could see bone.

-Pinch hard below the joint, Delroy said.

Greg did as told.

-Right, hold that.

He took his mouth to Greg's injured hand and

sucked at the gouge.

-What the fuck are you doin? Greg asked.

Delroy spat the blood he'd sucked into his empty mug.

-Dirt. Takes only one bit to infect the whole thumb, Delroy explained.

-Fuck off!

-Serious. Seen a lad lose his hand like that in the Army. Gangrene set in.

It can happen. Right. Hold the hand higher. Has the bleeding stopped yet?

-Almost.

-It needs stitching. Where are you going, Greg?

-Can't leave the fuckin' box hangin there, can we?

-Wait here. Let's get that bandaged then I'll finish it off.

Delroy fixed Greg's hand using the van's first aid kit, then completed the job. Greg wouldn't get it stitched and just wanted home. For the first time, Delroy drove the van while Greg sat in the passenger seat, his left hand swathed in a fresh bandage. He drove up Cherry Tree Estate, turning into Peach Avenue. Two snarling, short-arsed dogs chased their back wheels for a couple of houses. He parked up outside number 15.

-Nice place. You inviting me in for a cuppa?

-Like I can brew up with this going on?

-I'll do it for you.

-Nah, you're alright. You could drop the van off for me though. Larry's got some weekend jobs on.

-Alright, jump out then, mate, Delroy said.

-Catch you next week, Greg smiled. He waved Delroy off.

Delroy drove straight to Police Divisional HQ, the blood sample washing around his mug in the back of the van, and he had the first bandage blood too.

This time Hilary Meadows did not even extend his hand. They were sat either side of a table in another HQ office cube, empty except for the two of them. -I thought I told you not to visit here?

-I love a warm welcome.

-You've brought your own cup this time?

The mug he had spat Gregory's blood into was in his hand. He held it out.

-It's got his blood in it, he explained. He tabled the bandage too.

-I take it you refer to Gregory Gresty's blood?

-S'right.

-Maybe you can tell me how you obtained it?

Delroy explained. He paid no heed to the trace of amusement ghosting across Meadows' face. -DNA match it to the blood found on the victim and we're done and dusted.

Hilary Meadows did his head scratch routine.

-Well? Delroy asked. Aren't you at least going to thank me? Delroy watched Meadows carefully.

-You are so naive, it's unbelievable, Meadows said at last.

-I've been called many things, but naive's a first.

-This is exactly how to wreck a case. You did not obtain this sample legally. This sample gets in the system and the judge could throw the whole case out.

Meadows was enjoying himself now. He liked doom.

-Why is it not legal? Delroy queried.

-The law states we need reasonable cause to take a blood sample.

-This hasn't been taken. This has been given. He gave it to me. Now I'm giving it to you.

-You're a lawyer now? Everyone's a lawyer now.

-I'm stating the facts. Some cops were too procedural. For Delroy's money, Hilary Meadows was one of them.

-Nice try but it won't wash.

-Can't you test it anyway?

-No.

-Because?... A because is customary here.

-I already explained, if it enters the system, it leaves an audit trail. The Defence will have the right to know how we came by it. They'll go to the judge and get the case thrown out for procedural irregularity, unconscionable dealings. The best thing for you is to walk out that door carrying your grubby little cup of blood and bandage, and keep walking, forget you ever came with it.

Delroy sighed. Three types didn't get any turnout for their funerals: bookies, estate agents and desk cops. The Kray twin, bad fucker that he was, got a horse-drawn carriage and crowds.

-Wakey, wakey, you still with us? Meadows said.

-You won't do it, then?

-I'm doing you a favour here.

-That's a 'no'?

-There are legal ways to obtain a sample. Evidence must be come by legally.

-For example?

-Like after an arrest and charge. Or when the sample is specifically volunteered for the purpose, or after a road accident. You know the irony of this? I'm usually drilling procedure into thick police officer skulls. Isn't that what you people want? Things done properly?

-'You people'. You mean black people?

-Black. Green. Radical. Anarchist. Lesbian. Lefties.

Delroy drove back up the Old Burnham Road to

Aardvark. He conceded Meadows was more in the know on the regulations. What rankled? Something. The spring in Meadows' step when he had ushered him out? It seemed crazy Meadows not running a test to see if the blood matched. 'An absence of verifiable facts.' There were tens of thousands of registered white vans crawling around Burnham. Over three thousand of the Burnham electorate voted BNP at the local elections and everyone was getting tattooed nowadays.

The strangest thing was, there were moments when Delroy found himself wishing Meadows was right. He liked Greg. They had their laughs. The rats in the loft that had had them both scrambling like fuck for the ladders. The mill-house stone they had not been able to drill through where they had ended up bringing in two Acrow props and a sledgehammer, all to wire one outside box. And the karate class recruitment guy they had found doing chops in two different bedrooms on the Orange Grove estate: they'd hardly been able to hold onto their drills for laughing. There was a serious side to Greg too. His sudden, lonely mournfulness. He'd told him how, at his mother's funeral, his sisters had been bawling their eyes out and he hadn't shed one tear and to this day all he felt was numb about it. Fact was, there were times when Delroy felt protective towards him. No matter how off-the-scale a crime the guy had committed, there were always aspects of him he could relate to. It was Attachment Syndrome. He'd made the tag up himself. It had a ring to it. He should apply for a professorship somewhere.

11

Monday morning and rain poured out of the sky. A bullying wind blasted brickwork, drenched their tools, shot rain along overloaded gutters. They did the outside box fast then retreated inside.

Greg was in one of his moods. He kept the radio blaring.

There was something obscene about the local DJ with his 'Ha! Ha! Ha! Wonderful! Marvellous!' while outside the weather was murdering the earth.

-Shit weather, right? How's the hand healing?

-Larry wants to know what you were doing outside Central Police Station yesterday evening, Greg said.

-That's what you've been sulking about?

There was no response from Greg.

-What's it to Larry? he stalled.

-You were there then?

-Let me see, Larry sees a black man there and all black men look the same, right?

-Only one black man drives an Aardvark van.

Damn! -OK, you got me there, it was me. I got stopped, he said, as nonchalantly as he could manage, - Police thought I'd nicked the van. I told them 'ring and check' and they did, but they couldn't get through, you know how the office phone glows on Fridays. Anyway, something else comes up on the radio and they let me go with a Producer ticket, you know what one of them is? You have to produce your documents. That was why I was there. It happens regular if you're a black man with a half decent set of wheels.

Delroy was gambling on Greg not knowing too much about producers. The lad looked half convinced. He was sure Greg wanted to believe him, wouldn't want to chuck their growing friendship away all because of one sighting outside police HQ. Delroy wondered who had seen him. Probably one of the Aardvark workers, passing by.

Greg was about to say something when the house owner came in with a tray. It was one of their mutually agreed routines: the mid-morning tea break.

-Great timing, love. Cheers, ta, Delroy said to the owner.

She nodded. -Watch those covers, she said, then walked off.

They sat in the conservatory cane chairs, steaming and sipping.

-So you was a squaddie before this, right? Greg asked.

-For a while. Then I... He could not say he was homeless for a couple of years. He settled on something partially true. -... I was an extra in a film.

-You? In films?

-Sort of, Delroy shrugged. He had been living rough when some student film-makers had used him as an extra. He never saw the finished film, though they did buy him a hot dog for his trouble.

-What film was it? Greg said.

-Nothing Hollywood, he said modestly, -a student film, I played a dead body.

-No kiddin'? said Greg, his suspicion forgotten in that moment.

-It's true. Delroy decided to spin it, it would entertain Greg and him both:

-Thing is it's not easy being a dead body. Think about

it. When you die, your eyes stay open, right? That's science. Dead men don't blink. He demonstrated to a keenly listening Greg. -But try holding that pose while they're filming. It's not easy. So in this film I've fallen down dead and he's on his knees, the star that is. He pulls me, his best friend who's now the dead body, to his chest, saying, 'No! don't die on me!' right? Now it's only natural to look at someone who's talking to you, it's only polite, right? but you can't, 'cos you're dead, follow? So you've got to screen it out, look nowhere, but keep your eyes open. Remember Jack Nicholson in 'The Shining' when his wife whacked him and she's dragging him along the floor and his eyes go like this? Delroy flickered his eyes for effect.

-I didn't see it, but go on, Greg laughed.

-It was class, real dead body, or close-to-dead body acting. But then Jack's got an Oscar, I don't. There's your breathing as well to think about, you can't have your chest rising and falling, you know what I'm sayin'? Delroy imitated a dead body breathing absurdly.

Greg's smile spanned out.

-So it's difficult, right? But I had it pat. Director told me after I was the best dead body he ever worked with.

-You're a funny guy, man, Greg said.

-I does my best.

-Go on then.

-What?

-Be a dead body.

-Haven't you been listening? You can't do it just like that. You have to get into character.

Greg sucked his lower lip in, still smiling. -You're winding me up, he said. -You're full of shit, good shit, though.

They broke a couple of biscuits and dunked them in

their tea.

-Do you ever think about if there's anything other than this life, Sil? Greg started.

-Like if you keel over, do you move on to some Alarm Company in the sky?

-Right. Or is this it?

-You die, you're dead? Delroy finished for him. -Dunno. Guess we all find out in the end.

They got on with the job.

Mid-way through the afternoon, Hargreaves made a call to Greg's mobile. Although Delroy was in another room, he heard Greg say: 'No problems... we're fine, everything's pukka.' It was good to hear.

The rain had stopped and he was outside working on a box when there was a shout from the street:

-Mr Johnson! Mr Johnson! You found anything yet? Have you found anything?

A girl's voice, Asian face. It was the girl in the Amin house. Karim's little sister. They were not that so far from Karim's house. Hargreaves was having them work the area.

-Hey, sweetie, hush it up, hush it up! What are you, a radio station?

He came down the ladder. Greg was in the hallway choosing fixing bolts. Delroy opened the short, sprung iron gate and met the girl on the pavement.

She looked nervous, still surprised to see him and took a little step away as he stepped next to her.

-How are you, Samira?

-There's good days and bad days.

A sophisticated answer for a little girl. She looked up at him, hope brimming. -I wondered if, it's just that, you know... My dad and my brothers don't tell me much.

-There's not much to tell, Delroy said, -the police are working their angles, and, well, I'm working mine.

She laughed a nervous laugh. -I thought you'd given up, seeing you here up a ladder.

Delroy heard Greg's work boots moving up the path.

-Just helping a mate. He took a step closer and half whispered, -I don't want to be rude Samira, but let me call you, OK, I've got a job on here.

She was puzzled. She didn't understand, but he couldn't explain, with Greg almost at his shoulder.

-OK, she said, -you'll call then? And she backed away and was gone.

Greg was at his shoulder. -What was she yakking about?

-Her puppy. She used to live at the house back of mine, and lost it in my garden. I found her searching and said I'd keep an eye open. Girls and puppies, eh?

They wrapped the job up early and installed themselves in the conservatory again. Greg waxed on about the merits of Bosch over Black and Decker. Then, after a long, tired silence, Greg asked: -Why are we here on this earth? Ever thought of that, Sil?

-Dunno. To enjoy it?

-We're here, then we're gone: what's that about?

Delroy chuckled. -Sounds like a blues song.

-In the span of time, we're not here for even that. Greg snapped his fingers.

-All the more reason to party, Delroy said.

-Bollocks!

-Is it your girlfriend? You still taking the break up hard?

-What makes you thing we've broke up?

-You told me she said she never wanted to see you again in this life or the next?

-So?

-That pretty categorical, as brush-offs go.

-She's got a mouth on her, that's all. I just have to give her something to impress her, like and she'll come back.

-Chocolates? Flowers? A puppy?

Greg smiled, but his eyes narrowed.

-She's not the puppy kind of girl then?

Again Greg didn't answer. He could be stubbornly uncommunicative at times. -How's the football mates? They phoned you yet?

-They will. When a big match comes.

-Shagging one of your mate's girlfriends wasn't smart.

Delroy was trying to provoke him. There was something stirring in Greg and he wanted to catch it.

-Fuck them... They're afraid, Greg said.

-Of what? Delroy waited.

-Nothing, Greg said finally.

-Right, that makes sense... Of you?

-... Sort of.

-Why?

-... You ever done anything bad, Sil?

-I've pulled the legs off a few spiders in my time. How about you?

-Let's go, Greg said, suddenly standing. -I'll drop you off, he added magnanimously.

-It's no trouble.

-Listen man, I insist. I wanna see this garden of lost puppies you've got.

So he had not forgotten. -OK, let's go, said Delroy.

He had Greg drive onto an estate he knew. He told him to pull over next to a house with a garden of weeds and a short fence made of pallet wood.

-You want to come in? Delroy asked casually. *It was a huge gamble.*

-Another time, Greg said.

Delroy got out of the van and waved Greg off. Greg raised the palm of his hand in acknowledgement, but instead of putting the van in gear, he began fiddling with his mobile phone. *What to do?* thought Delroy. He looked up the path at the front door of the house he'd chosen. In the house front window a red-haired young woman with a nappied child in her arm was looking back at him through her scalloped, French net curtain.

Delroy took a step towards her wooden gate. *Now what?*

If he put a hand on the gate she might blast him. People defended their territory fast these kind of places.

He looked back at Greg. He was still thumbing his phone.

He took another step towards the gate. The woman's outline came closer to the net. Any moment, she was going to swish that net back and shout something.

Was Greg stalling? He was cagey and smart. Delroy bent down, fiddling with his left shoelace. This was desperate. A man in worn brown Hush Puppies, centre creased, nylon grey trousers, a walnut walking stick, a thin black overcoat and slicked silver hair came towards him. Delroy bobbed up when the old man was two steps before him.

-Fancy seeing you again! he cried.

The man stopped, startled.

-Blackpool a couple of years back, remember? Eric isn't it?

Her seemed more amused than afraid. He waved to the woman behind the net curtain but indulged Delroy:

-George actually. Did we meet, fella? he said.

-You got on great with my wife, you old charmer, George. Sheila, remember, or are you like that with all the ladies?

He blushed.

-Blackpool, only in Blackpool! You goin' this year?

-I'm a granddad again, can't afford it. Five now, five girls an' all. His chest swelled with pride.

-Congratulations! Delroy said, holding out his hand.

Swapping his walnut walking stick from his right to his left, the old man took Delroy's outstretched hand. Delroy held it and held on. He took another glance at Greg. He was finally putting his phone down.

-And what are their names, George? Delroy said, keeping hold of the man's hand.

-Ah well, there's Rebecca, there's Georgie, there's...

-Georgie! Named after you?

-That's right!

-You lucky fella!

-And there's Gemma, there's Tiffany, there's...

Greg and the van finally took off.

Delroy released the old man's hand. It had been a longer handshake than Castro would have give Marx.

-I'm visitin' our Linda as it happens. You want to come in for a cuppa? George asked.

Delroy made his excuses as politely as he could.

Evening fell fast. At Trudy's flat, after they had eaten they watched television on the sofa together. Then they went to bed and slept, or at least tried.

He felt her startle.

-You OK?

-It's nothing.

-Can I get you an aspirin?

-Rest back, I'm fine... I like it when he's kicking, even

if he hits the fibroid, it means he's alive. She took his hand and placed it on her bulge. -Can you feel him kicking?

-Yup.

-Sometimes he's turning somersaults... I need a two-bedroom now. I phoned Giselle at the Housing and they'll definitely move us soon as something suitable comes in. I have lists of clothes, lists of nurseries... My sister's coming down from London this weekend. She thinks I should have a water birth, what do you think?...

-Can you swim?

-Seriously.

-Sounds OK.

-It's supposed to be less stressful. He'll be born like a dolphin, paddle up to the surface. 'Hi world, I'm borned!'... What are you thinking about?

-Nothing.

Delroy's thoughts were not thoughts Trudy would have appreciated. How could he be sure the baby was his? There had been other men she was seeing at the time, she said they were friends of friends and he mostly trusted her, but a man never knew whether a child was his or not except by a DNA result. He'd even heard of a baby being the spit of a guy, everyone said it even his own mother, and then the test showed it couldn't be his, it turned out to be his brother's. The family street fight took a Transit of police to damp down.

-I know you're lying there fretting about something... I don't mind if you're at the birth or not.

-It's this case. I don't know if it's going anywhere.

-Have they paid you?

-Yes, upfront.

She sat up. -I know you don't tell me everything but you let too much things drift. Some people get comfortable drifting then things kick off and it's 'I didn't see that coming' when all along it was there, jumping around on the horizon and they should have been paddling like mad one way or the other, but they chose to drift.

She waited for a response from him. He was not offering any.

-... Take your debts.

-Go ahead, take them, Delroy groaned, turning on his side, away from her. She was not going to sleep, that much was clear.

-Instead of owing Flat Jimmy, and Rosie, and Han, you could pay them all off and just owe one amount to a bank. It's called money management.

-But that would dampen my popularity.

-Please?

-When you owe people enough they treat you nice, they've got an interest in your welfare and future prosperity.

She did not see the humour. -Flat Jimmy won't be fobbed off forever.

-How do you know about my debts anyway?

-You're not the only one can find out things.

-They're no big deal. I'm making the instalments, everyone's happy.

-I just think you need organising. I know you're not a list person, but...

-We're not going to sleep, are we? Delroy said, turning on his side again, this time towards her. -Thing is, Trude, I like to let things develop, see where they go. He ran a hand along her thigh under the quilt.

She didn't resist. -I guess that approach can have its moments, she said.

He felt her lips smiling under his hand as he licked

her shoulder.

It was the Monday of his final trial week at Aardvark. They worked on a series of vacant terraced properties, owned by a DSS landlord hiding behind a company nameplate. One house to the next, it was all the same: beige emulsion that had not dried at the foot of the lounge walls because of damp, ham-fisted wiring into wall sockets and light fittings, and kitchen units with soaking rear panels from leaking pipes.

At dinnertime, Greg wanted to take some time off to pay a few bills. He asked Delroy to cover.

-Course, can't let the bosses work us to death.
-You'll be OK?
-Scram.

Greg made it back around three pm.

The property where they finished up for the day was the worst and they had been warned about it. The back garden was a jungle of wild bushes, sodden, collapsed woodchip furniture, old settees and rotting carpet. A blue, high-sided plastic tub had flies swirling round it and generated a stink that reached every room in the house. Inside the house, plastic window frames buckled where lintels had failed, not a single window or door closed properly. The carpets all crawled with woodlice and larvae. There was a Belling electric cooker hard wired to the mains. The house was a death trap, but they got on and did the job they were there to do.

Greg kept his radio ramped up all afternoon. Delroy knew he was nursing something. Finally, as they finished up and sank into a mouse-chewed settee, Greg unloaded:

-That police producer ticket?
-What about it, Greg, lad?

-You get fourteen days to bring in your papers.

Greg had carried it all this time, Delroy realised. -Just thought I'd get it done, you know, then knock back a few drinks. Better that way round, if you think about it.

Greg did not answer but Delroy could see him chewing on it. They were sitting in the lounge facing the rear windows. With the boards down, they could see straight into the jungle at the back. -Get the bills paid?

Greg curled his lip upward in a yes.

-Some house, right? Delroy said.

Greg grunted assent.

There was silence again. Greg began looking at him, surreptitiously scrutinising him.

-What? asked Delroy, protesting.

-You could easily die here and disappear, he said.

-Come again? The conversation had just nudged into the macabre.

-Well, it's like this. Thousands of people disappear every year, you see their pictures in the *Big Issue*, the ones someone's looking for, like. Most of them don't even get that.

-I guess.

-Take yourself.

-Take me.

-Let's say we had an accident in here and you copped it.

-That'd be easy. Switch on the cooker back there'd do anyone.

-What would I do?

-Switch off at the fuse box?

-Too late. You're dead. I roll your body in some of that carpet out there and dump it at the bottom of the garden...Who'd go looking for you out there?

-Nobody's going back there without a rotovator, a

face mask, and a full tank of oxygen.

-See?

-See what?

-You could disappear.

Delroy joked it away. -You'll have to brew up now, star, I'm not going near that cooker.

Greg was insistent. -You get my point? Go on. Who would come looking for you?

-Don't rub it in.

-Nobody. Makes you a prime target for a killer.

It sounded neither like a joke nor the over-earnest speculation young people loved. It was a disinterested assessment. If Greg had killed Karim, unless he was a complete psychopath, and Greg wasn't that, he would want to talk about it at some point. Was that what was doing? Or was it more than that? Was Greg quietly threatening him? Whatever it was, they were on the subject, and Delroy saw his chance.

-You hear about that Paki got killed in the alleyway by Freeham? he said.

-Got stuck with a knife, didn't he? Greg responded quickly.

-People say it was a mugging but I don't think so.

He saw Greg tense.

-Mugging happens on a High Street, continued Delroy, speaking easily, -near a cash till, or close. This was in the back of beyond.

-Suppose.

-... Whoever did it deserves a medal.

Relief skated over Greg's face.

-Thought you'd be soft on them, he said.

-What's Asians ever done for me? Delroy replied, -Give all blacks a bad name don't they, with their fiddling, smuggling. *God, what was he saying?* -Cops are not gonna bust their arses solving a case like that, are they? Stands to reason.

-Right. Another'll be through in the back of a lorry before you can say 'Channel Tunnel', Greg joked. -One less asylum seeker, he added.

Delroy joined in. He had to. -Never gonna open a corner shop now is he?

-Never gonna build a mosque! ...Whoever did it, they was taking the piss, wasn't they? Greg said. His eyes strayed over to Delroy.

-How's that? said Delroy.

-Leaving that cross in his hand. Gotta be taking the piss.

Delroy didn't blink. Was Greg testing him? He knew the meaning, but he was steady. He had to be steady. -Right... You think he worries about it?

-Who?

-Whoever did it?

-No way. He's laughing, Greg said.

-Right, he's bound to be laughing, Delroy agreed.

The day could not end quickly enough. Delroy took a taxi straight over, dialling as he travelled. He got the usual runaround from Meadows' office that he was out, off-base, at a meeting. He jumped out of the taxi at the rear of the building and entered via the fire door where the smokers gathered, using the rear stairwell. He phoned Meadows again from First, let him know he was coming to him, whether he wished it or not.

-I'm knocking on doors, here, someone's bound to direct me.

He heard Meadows curse him before conceding. -By the vending, then. Five minutes.

At the vending machine he gave Meadows a desultory handshake and a twenty-pence piece for his cappuccino. Meadows ushered him into a small office. -This is the last time.

Delroy stirred his coffee with a finger. -They shorted me on the froth.

-I had to leave an important meeting for froth?

-It's the Amin case.

-You're still on that?

-Right, nobody's been arrested have they?

-We've set the traps. We've even pulled officers from Traffic. We'll catch him, as soon as he strikes again.

-Won't that be too late?

-Defer to our experience. This is the way to go.

-Maybe, maybe not. Something in Delroy's manner slowed Meadows: -What have *you* got? he asked.

-He mentioned the cross.

-You've lost me.

-Karim was holding a cross in his hand? Delroy said.

-Well?

-Greg Gresty knows about it.

-And?

-That cross is not public knowledge, you didn't release it. How could he know unless..?

Meadows was silent for a moment. -It could have leaked, he said, but he was interested. -Did you record this conversation?

-No.

-Then you've got nothing. A simple denial from Gresty will kill it. In CPS eyes, there's nothing there. It wouldn't be heard in court. Hearsay rules. That coffee good?

-Are you serious?

-A prosecution hanging on the hearsay testimony of

an alcoholic, Army drop-out, freelance investigator currently sleeping out of a car? I don't think so.

-I'm making this up then?

-I'm saying the CPS will be professionally obliged to factor in such an idea.

-Do you believe me?

-My job's not to offer a speculative opinion. I'm here to sift and qualify...

-Your answer's you're not concerned, right?

-There's concerned, and there's running around like a rat on fire.

Delroy shifted his chair back. -Fuck it, Hilary. Forget I ever walked in.

Meadows stood with him. -Your first good idea, Delroy.

-And Mr Johnson, Meadows said as he reached the door, -next time you've got information, use the phone, like every fucking one else!

It was fucked up world. What was the use?

At Trudy's, he took a shower once he got the hang of the rubber hose thing that attached to the bath taps. The water was good. He wanted to sluice Meadows out of his skin, sluice Greg too. The stuff with Greg ran rough through his mind as the scalding shower bit into him. Was he encouraging him to commit another crime, the way they had talked? He climbed carefully out of the bath and towelled himself dry with the only towel.

-You're going to feel dirty, Trudy said when he told her the current situation, -it's not good talking that shit.

-You misunderstand, I was in a situation. He was massaging her shoulders on the sofa, and she was lecturing him. That was gratitude.

-No, I hear it all the time, and from black people too. That's what makes me laugh, no-one thinks it through.

'Right, let's get all the migrants removed,' they say. Abracadabra. Done. What then? No-one to clean your toilets at the office, no-one buffing your corridor floors, no-one driving your taxi home, no-one cooking your dinner at the take-away, and in the sweat-shop factories no-one stuffing the pillow you push under your head when you go to sleep, no Security guarding your gate in the dead of the night so you've got a job to go to when you wake up again; don't get injured, you won't have a doctor; don't get ill, you won't have a nurse neither. That's what they want?

It was like massaging a block of wood. -Lean back. You're not meant to get stressed, remember? he said.

-Don't 'calm' me.

-OK. Now relax, breathe, let it go... Good.

-I feel for them, you know, that's what.

-Who?

-The people that lost their son.

-Right.

-And I, I mean, if you stopped dithering, you know? and started being more effective...

-It's my fault now? What's this 'effective'?

-Either you do something or it looks like you're taking them for their money. And the Amins don't need that, on top of everything.

Delroy smiled to himself at the money idea. He'd earned hardly a baked bean on this job. With expenses, he was well into minus. She got up from under his hands. -Where are you going? he called.

-I made some juice. She came back with two glasses and a jug of real lemon juice. He watched her walk cumbersomely over to the table in the corner and put them down. Somehow she knew he was watching her.

-Yes, I waddle now, I'm a pregnant frog. She sat

down at the table. -And if the lift goes, that's it, I'll have to live off tins.

-Any time, just call and I'll bring stuff, he said. -Come here. He wanted her under his hands gently.

-Like... ackees, Polish rye bread, Jacob's mango pickle? she said, coming over.

-You text it, I'll bring it.

She sat down again between his knees and he started working her shoulders gently.

-Do you want to know if it's a girl or a boy? she said.

It always caught him how she switched like that. From one thing to something a solar system beyond, without a breath in between.

-I thought they didn't tell you, he replied.

-They did another scan because of the fibroid.

-Doing somersaults you said? Got to be a boy.

She laughed. -You have a little girl on the way.

He kissed the back of her neck.

-... I'll have to learn where the pink zone is at Mothercare, and how to plait hair. How to organise sleep-overs, she said.

-Then how to fend off boyfriends, he chipped in.

He helped clear the dishes away, again watching her. Her hair was a little mushed and her bare feet left ghost tracks on the floor when she walked. And as he watched her, he thought: she was spoiling him. They had worked through a pot of rice, spare ribs in barbecue sauce, and real lemon juice with the pips floating, and with ice, all his favourites.

Dishes done, they lay on the sofa, she resting the side of her head on his stomach, and they slumbered there until the chill set in, then they drifted across to bed.

Trudy snored, mouth open, in the land of dreams. Delroy waited for sleep. He followed the swirled stipple paint on her ceiling, done with a wide emulsion brush, he guessed. Life was good. Anywhere else – his church office, his car, Susan's – the cold would be sinking through to his bones; but right here, right now, with Trudy heating the bed better than a Bermuda Baxi and the local dogs finally done with their yapping, and the woman above kicked off her high heels, a kind of peace had descended. It was an elusive thing, like finding a decent Fiat clutch in a breaker's yard, or a condom machine in Vatican City: you could chase after peace as hard as you wanted and never find it, and even if you did, it had a habit of ghosting away, gone no sooner it was sighted, the way a raindrop melted when it hit the surface of a river, lost forever in the river.

He waited, but still no sleep came. He had three working days left at Aardvark. He had enough but Meadows held out. He was exhausted with Meadows. Meanwhile he risked discovery by Greg. He'd had enough scares already. The HQ sighting. The drop-off when he was standing there waving at Greg, tying his shoelace. How stiff was that? And Samira. He had managed to settle Greg over her at the time, but he knew Greg's nature, he would be turning it over, somewhere in Greg's mind he was onto him. That stuff this afternoon in the conservatory about how if he killed him no-one would know. It was a joke and it was not. It was hanging in the air. Anyone who had killed once, could kill again. Statistics, as Meadows would say. He should walk away, leave it to the cops, however fucked their approach. Trudy needed him, his baby needed him. People had never needed him like this before, it was fresh territory. He twisted and turned.

Trudy woke suddenly and sat up: -You'll have to give up your other women, she said blankly. -Don't think I don't know about them, and I'm not having it.

-Go back to sleep, he chided, half-heartedly. He welcomed her disturbance of his thoughts.

She sat up stubbornly, perfectly asleep, yet perfectly conscious too in her own crazy way.

He sat up with her. -... Would you come looking for me if I went missing? he asked.

-With sniffer dogs, she snorted. And her head tucked right into the pillow again.

He watched her twitch and sigh. She was beautiful. He was not smart with women. He was always in some tangle or other. His clothes, or most of them, were still with Susan. Meanwhile, Violet the church woman was lighting candles for him down the road. And here he was, sleeping in Trudy's bed. Trudy said he was drifting; he liked to drift, but it was more complicated than that. Violet had arranged the office for him and he had not liked to discourage her. To suddenly break off their time together would be a betrayal, the same as admitting he had misled her over the office. Susan and he had been over for some time, and it was only he didn't want a screaming match that kept him from going there and collecting his stuff. This drifting, Trudy broad-brushed it Forth Bridge style, to everything in his life: the baby situation, their relationship, the job he was on. Was it an unfair accusation? He drifted to sleep.

12

Wednesday morning was foul: squalls and thunder. He went straight to the first address. Greg was there already and Delroy told him he had a funeral to attend, and would he cover for him, he would be back by four pm? Greg muttered an OK.

Did he buy it? Delroy had to believe.

He took the Wolverhampton train. He looked out of the train window. Clouds floated like scum on a river weir, backing up in the sky, ready to dash down in torrents onto the roofs below. The train charged on. Behind the clouds struggled a weak light, like a torch with a half-dead battery. Eventually the rain burst down, raking the train carriage, blasting the roof.

Delroy shifted in his seat, uncomfortable. It seemed to him the train companies were in competition with each other to see who could make the narrowest, shallowest chairs with the least legroom between. He had wedged himself into an aisle seat, that way he could still stretch his legs along the aisle even if someone sat next to him. In the window versus aisle debate, he was always aisle, he mused. He felt weary. Something heavy hung over him that he could not grab, ghosts stirring that he would rather didn't wake. He was dressed all in black. It had been to cover himself with Greg. For what he was about to do, it might not be perfect, he thought; he did not want to look too Mafiosi. He fished his silver necklace out of a jacket pocket and slipped it on, then checked his reflection in the train window. The chain stood out against the funeral black of his shirt. A weary gangster figure looked back at him. He took the chain off.

This job had drained him. Now it was about to drain the last of his money. He had not contacted the Amin family or Wasif because there was nothing to contact them with. Was Meadows cautious or intransigent? It did not matter now. If a mountain could not be moved, you simply steered round it.

As the train pulled further south the weather eased. He'd visited Wolverhampton to see friends years ago, old army friends. He was tempted to do a surprise visit to one or two of them but army types were restless and they would all have moved on now, either squadding at some overseas posting or else simply moved. Besides, who liked those kind of surprises nowadays? When he finally got off at Wolverhampton station, he used his *A-Z* to work his way through the city to his destination, surprised at the changes he saw. It was one of those ugly-beautiful cities. And it had grown uglier and more beautiful in equal parts. He did not stand around, he was not a tourist and he did not want to feature big on the city's CCTV. He checked his map, then headed on.

Off a street close to a McDonald's on the outskirts of south Wolverhampton spread the sprawling used-car zone called Wolverhampton National Car Auctions. Delroy stood across the road from it and admired all the glinting metal and glass. The official auctions were going on in there. On his side of the street stood freelancers' cars, parked up nose to nose and ready for sale, all with scrawled mobile phone numbers on cardboard strips in the dashes. Bumper to bumper, these less pampered vehicles went the length of the road, for some quarter of a mile, skipping here and there onto grass verges and under advertising hoardings. Delroy worked his way along the road until he found the closest to what he required. A 'P' reg, old model Ford Mondeo. It was jammed three-quarters onto the pavement and pedestrians had to brush past it. He checked his watch. 1.16 p.m. He guessed hundreds of people would have touched it as they had gone past; and even today a dozen potential punters would have ducked inside and grabbed hold of the steering wheel while reading the mileage. He liked the look of it. He dialled the mobile phone number in the windscreen.

A 'Dennis' answered, told him to wait, he'd do him a good deal and appeared by his side within two minutes of the call. 'Dennis' had quick eyes and a warm, bony hand; his nose had pink imprints either side where glasses had once rested. He looked gaunt, and ashen, probably from the Balkans, at least Albanian, maybe on a mission to make some hard-earned and send it home fast. He wore a black zip fleece jersey one size too big and polycotton light trousers, mottled at the ankles with mud.

-Is there a log book? Delroy asked.

'Dennis' smiled. -Here? No log books. There is log books. 'Dennis' pointed over at the Wolverhampton NCA auction site.

To ordinary buyers no log book was a negative, but not to Delroy. He pulled on his gloves and looked around the car some more, lifted the bonnet.

-... Passed by the AA, 'Dennis' threw in.

Delroy glanced at him with a raised eyebrow.

-Armed Anonymous.

-Sorry?

-Excuse. My private joke.

Maybe he did look like an armed robber, Delroy thought. The black he was wearing and now the gloves.

All he needed was a ski mask.

-She's a good runner, 'Dennis' grinned.

There had to be a manual of car sellers' patter somewhere. Maybe it was part of the citizenship test: how to speak car sales talk.

'Dennis' watched him as he looked the Mondeo over comprehensively. The tyres were fair, though worn on the front inner side. The shocks were shot at the rear and the car was listing to the left, the windows did not wind, there was welding on the back axle, the number plates had new anchor screws, there were fresh etchings on the engine block and no VIN panels on the inside door where the VIN number should have been; the air bag and casing were gone and you did not use a key to start it.

-Can you start the engine? Delroy asked.

'Dennis' held the two ignition wires together and Delroy went round and listened. There was a tapping coming from the camshafts, and the carburettor was stuttering at low revs, but otherwise it was OK. Working his way round again, Delroy had to smile. A mint tax disc shone proudly on the windscreen, its ink barely dry. The car was either a knock-off or a write-off, or most likely both. A car with history. Just what he wanted. He double-checked the brake pipes and the brakes. It was a runner. It was not going to harry the BMWs in the M6 fast lane to Burnham, but should manage a steady trot along the A-roads, he decided.

-Very nice car, 'Dennis' said closing in.

-Can I see it on the road?

-Sure, I drive, you watch.

'Dennis' got a red, plastic fuel can from the back seat of another car along the road and sloshed some fuel in the Mondeo's tank. He pulled the car out and drove it up, then down the road with a smile, even waved to Delroy as he passed. It sounded rough but OK, Delroy thought. 'Dennis' bumped it smoothly back up the kerb.

-It's got a radio?

'Dennis' flipped the glove compartment down. There was a cheap battery-powered radio in there. Delroy smiled again.

-She's a real goer. Diesel, don't worry about the mileage.

-I'll take it for 150. The cardboard sign had asked for two hundred.

-Please, I have to make money.

-140.

-You are robbing my hand off.

-130.

-150. This business is useless, I should dig potatoes, 'Dennis' complained, but Delroy guessed 150 meant a hundred clear profit for 'Dennis'.

They shook on the deal.

-I could vac over it for you?

-No, I'll take it as is. The filthier the better, Delroy was thinking. That way Forensics could either spend a year collecting hairs off the seat, mud from the tyres, fibres from the boot, and prints from the cockpit that half the population of Wolverhampton had walked through, or, more likely, they would give it up as a waste of resources.

'Dennis' counted the cash with a smack of each note, the way those in the cash economy loved to. It was Thin Harry's payment for the month that 'Dennis' was fingering. Something else would turn up to pay Thin, Delroy thought; right now, he needed this car. He ducked into the driver's seat. 'Dennis' appeared at the window. He opened the door to hear him.

-Remember, the needle very low if you drive far, 'Dennis' said, pointing to the gauge.

The guy was smart. Delroy gave him an extra twenty to fill the Mondeo with red diesel. That done, he jammed the wires together. The engine started with a splutter. In his off-side mirror, Delroy saw 'Dennis' disappear behind an advertising hoarding. Neither of them had ever seen the other before, nor would they know each other from Adam if asked subsequently by the police, he was sure. He put the Mondeo in gear and took off.

Small towns straggled by. His body heat soon fogged the windows. The side windows were either fully up or fully down, no in-between. He drove with the driver's side down and passenger's up. A squall of rain drenched him and blanked the windscreen until the wipers miraculously started slashing away. He tried to keep in the general direction of north, using the twisting A and B roads. He went through a forest with gnarled, straggly trees, and then another forest with straight, tall trees. The rain steadied, and it became easier to drive, the drops merging to form a lake on the screen that he could see through without the erratic wipers. The radiator temperature gauge was creeping up.

He crossed a town. On the road out, traffic queued behind him. He was doing 40, they wanted to do 50. He waved them on: he needed to reach Burnham with the Mondeo still a goer. He got horns, wanker signs as they overtook, but he paid no heed, nursed the Mondeo on. Gear shifting was the trickiest because of the worn clutch. He switched down to second at the first sign of an incline. Driving a sound car was a doddle compared with run-ins. Fortunately, if that was the right word, he had had plenty of experience with run-ins.

He stopped at a trucker's lay-by for a burger and tea from a caravan café, and to allow the radiator gauge to climb down. The tea buckled the thin plastic cup and burnt his tongue. He made it back to Burnham without incident.

Greg was finishing up in a flat in Bonsall Road, Leemouth, when Delroy phoned him. Delroy parked the Mondeo in a side road close to the Dog and Partridge then made his way over, reaching at 5.15pm, mindful he had to do his utmost to make what needed to happen, happen.

-You're late, Greg noted, when he had crossed the flat's threshold. It was an empty flat, recently replastered.

-Sorry. Black people's funerals always run late, Delroy joked.

Greg did not catch the humour. He was shooting floorboards with a nail gun, making a messy row of nails.

-You want to get the nail heads flush, Delroy advised.

Greg looked up. -Yeah? As he lifted his head up, he pointed the nail gun straight at Delroy's gut. His finger was on the trigger. -Who's funeral was it? Greg asked, not moving.

-Mother of a friend of a friend, Delroy said, turning slightly sideways. If the gun went off, it gave Greg less of a target.

-Let's see the invite then.

-I got a phone call, last night. Cancer.

-What hymns d'you sing?

-The usual, Delroy said, relaxing, feigning that he was remembering, feigning also that he had not noticed the pointed gun. –'Amazing Grace', 'Sleep The Divine

Sleep'. That kind of stuff. The whole town turned out to see her off. He did not know if 'Sleep The Divine Sleep' was a hymn, but he guessed Greg would not know either.

The gun lowered, -Yeh, right. Greg was sceptical, but he went back to nailing the floorboards.

-What's the matter? A customer been pissing you off? Delroy tried.

-Someone's been pissing me off.

The comment was directed at him. Greg was looking dangerous.

Delroy watched from the doorway as Gregory nailed in the last floorboard. When he was done he called out: -C'mon, Dog and Partridge.

-Dunno.

-I'm buying, lad.

They went there, in the van, Greg at the wheel. He asked more questions about the funeral. Delroy simply used the last funeral he had attended as the basis for his answers. They were heading for the pub, that was what mattered to him. The plan was still on track.

At the bar, Greg was still quizzing him on the funeral.

-I'll get the drinks in, said Delroy magnanimously. -Why are you so interested in funerals: you been asked to arrange one?

-You could say that, yeah.

-Go sit down, you're acting weird, man.

Greg went off to a corner seat. Delroy glanced around. There were only a few customers, mostly the regular drunks who only ever saw the end of their glasses, and a few tradesmen. A jukebox started playing some Metal screech. Delroy had to shout at the bar to make himself heard:

-Hold the rum!
-Just blackcurrant?
-That's right.

He brought the drinks over to Greg at the table and sat alongside him. Greg quaffed his Stella with impressive speed. Before he could protest, Delroy got him another. The booze took some of the edge out of Greg's manner. In its place came a surly hostility.

-I know who you are. Greg tapped Delroy's shoulder with an accusing finger.

-Go on. Lord Lucan?

-No.

-An African Prince pretending to be a pauper?

-Nope.

-Well, kiss me if I am, I'm ready to wake up.

Greg shook his head, unimpressed. -... You're a cop, he said with certainty.

Delroy laughed. -They'll be laughing in the police cells, hearing that.

-All the time pretending to be my best friend. I trusted you an' all.

Delroy stayed convivial. -What brings this on?

-You don't live at that house, I went an' asked. And you was never going in for a producer, that's not the place. And the boss only took you on 'cos he's paying you nowt. He's got no address on you and you give him no ID. You're a man without a shadow.

-'Without a shadow'? I like that.

-Means one thing. You're a cop.

-You finished?

-God, I must've been thick not to have noticed before.

-That is the biggest heap of shit I've heard since the Princess Diana conspiracies.

-I see through you, Sylvester, if that's your real name. You don't fool me.

Delroy charged on, weaving his story. He had to make it good. -You're right on the house. I live in a church room and, what the fuck, I'm embarrassed: man of my age living out of a sleeping bag on a church floor.

-I am not a total muggins, Greg said.

Delroy segued on. -Why? A man of my age living off church charity?

Greg stared at him.

-Alright, I do have police connections, but it's not how you think. I'm on probation. Get it? He leaned into Greg. -You're the only person I've told. If it leaks I know where it comes from.

Greg leaned away, his head shaking. -Nah, I'm not having it.

Delroy held up his thumb and index finger in a sign. -I am that close to getting a real job, all I need is the reference from fuckin' Hargreaves. Nobody gives an ex con a job, right? And that's why I lied to your boss. It isn't easy on the outside; there's old associates from the criminal fraternity I have to avoid from time to time. Means the occasional duck and dive, understand, like today?

-It's all bull. You're a cop and that's that.

-That's your opinion?

-It's the truth.

-Too bad. What if I am a cop? What've you got to worry about? You rob some old lady and leave her in a ditch? You do that Paki in? Bet that's it, bet you did that Paki in?

Greg smiled knowingly. -You'll be wearing a wire an' all. Fuckin' hell, now I see it, it's so simple. And I nearly fell for it.

-Greg, you dumb fuck, you're vexing me with this shit. He stood. -Pat me down, see if I got wires on my tits and coming out of my arse. C'mon, what are you waiting for? He held his hands high, waiting for Greg to pat him down. Greg ignored the gesture. Delroy sat down again.

-You did that Paki, so fucking what? But me a cop? C'mon. That'd make sense – 'put a black cop onto a white guy who kills Pakis'. Like the white guy ain't gonna see him coming from a mile. Nah. You're gettin' paranoid, Greg. You've got to get out more.

-You're a cop. And I'm gonna do something about it.

-Like what, Greg? Stab me, like how you stabbed up the Paki?

-Maybe.

-Like you fancy your chances, Greg, eh? You got a knife on you right now? Eh, Gregory?

Greg turned and jabbed a finger in Delroy's face: -Don't you fuckin' 'Gregory' me, you shit-faced fucker! You're a Fuckin' Nigger Cop!

It was that moment for Delroy. The tingle on the edge of his skin. The sour smell in his nose. The lungs braced. The thumping blood in the neck. 'Strangle the bastard' running through his mind. They were eyeball to eyeball. He felt the vortex swirling, sucking him into the big bang of violence.

Delroy stepped back. -Fuck this. Know what? Do what the fuck you want, Gregory. I'm out of here. I don't take shit like this from no-one. Understand? No-one!

He turned and walked for the door.

-Fuck off! Cop! I'll have you, wait and see! Greg called, victoriously.

Delroy made his exit.

It was time now to end this. The job was almost over.

He had his kit ready in the boot of the Mondeo and took it out: a grey, Reebok plastic hooded top, grey plastic Reebok bottoms, the gloves and some black frame glasses that he'd knocked the glass out of. He put them on. He went to the phone box, one hundred yards from the Dog and dialled the local police station where he knew they did not record, and reported a drunk driver, driving a white van erratically around West Burnham.

Then he returned to his Mondeo.

Delroy sat in the car and waited, keeping his head down. He calculated Greg would have one more pint then move. There was light traffic on the street. The sky was the dark, metallic blue it reached just before complete darkness. A guard dog barked in a back yard somewhere close, then was silent.

Sixteen minutes on, Delroy saw the unmistakable shadow of Gregory Gresty head towards the Aardvark van parked outside the Dog and Partridge.

He readied himself. He started the Mondeo. The van's left indicator flashed. He watched the van move off, begin its loop round through the one-way system. Even drunk, Gresty was tidy. Delroy reversed into an alley and turned the Mondeo round for the junction. Then waited. He checked his seat belt. He saw the van start its run along the one-way street. Game on.

He slipped the Mondeo into second and hit the accelerator hard. It picked up through to forty. He kept his right foot hard down on the accelerator. Three seconds. He would hit him driver's side on, in three seconds tops. This was stupid. This was risking his life. What about his baby? Then he was in the vortex again.

This time not stepping back. Plummeting, a willed charge into the maw of death.

He screamed. -Fuckin bastaaarrrd!

It meant himself. It meant Gresty. It meant Meadows. It meant God, Himself.

The boom of metal on metal.

Greg's face turning in panic, uncomprehending.

The Mondeo's windscreen jolted and splintered.

The van door's soft crumple.

The Mondeo engine's whine.

The van's lurch. Then topple. Going over on its side.

Scraping, sparks like a giant angle-grinder on the street.

Calmly, Delroy unclipped his seat belt and levered himself out of the car. He went round to the front of the overturned van. Gresty was trapped in the driver's seat. There was shattered glass and blood all over his face. His legs were jammed. His head was in the foot well, twisted to one side. He was muttering: 'Please save me! Please save me!

His seat belt had saved him. And Delroy was glad of that, despite everything, he hadn't wanted to kill him, one death was enough.

He could hear the patrol car's siren nearing. The traffic police would take charge of the scene. Drink driving was a recordable offence. They would formally arrest him, and obtain samples of his blood and saliva. Crash investigators could also take blood from the dashboard when they impounded the van. The samples would enter the database and throw up a result on the Amin case. It was what Meadows had stipulated: samples obtained by legal means by competent, recognised authorities with a clear, unbroken chain of possession.

In an alley, Delroy quickly stripped off the plastic track suit and the glasses and bundled them together in a bag. The patrol car arrived first. Then a fire engine. A black fireman stepped down from the engine's cab and hauled out cutting gear. Fate had a way of arranging these things.

Delroy walked away. The job was done.

Life was a river, and there was a time when it had been plain sailing for him on that river. Then the rocks had hit, and he'd been clinging to driftwood. He had learned to look onwards, outwards, not back. He was not doing too bad. He had direction now. He and Trudy, they had a direction.